If Cody knew her s
her? Hailey is afra

She stared up at him; there was nowhere else to look. His collar was open, the sleeves of his shirt rolled to his elbows. His voice was low and husky when he finally spoke. "Talk to me, Hailey."

She fought the tears. "I. . .can't." She tried to push past him but he didn't move, so she backed away from him, against the cupboard.

"Talk to me." The softness in his voice broke her. It was everything she ached for, and everything she couldn't have.

"I can't!" She screamed it. "I can't!" The sobs tore from her, and she slid to the floor. Then, somehow, she was cradled in Cody's arms, curled on his lap like a child, as he rocked her slowly, whispering in her hair.

"It's okay, Hailey. I know, and it's okay."

"You *don't* know, and you *can't* know," she sobbed into his shoulder.

Garment of Praise

Becky Melby
Cathy Wienke

Heartsong Presents

To every little girl's first hero and love, her dad:
Gerald C. Schwenn and to Phyllis J. Schwenn for her
care, guidance, and example.
Cathy

To my mother, Edie Foght,
for giving me life and teaching me love,
and to Kristen for letting us "borrow" your wedding
dress and especially. . .for loving my son.
Becky

A note from the Author:
I love to hear from my readers! You may write to me at
the following address: **Becky Melby & Cathy Wienke**
Author Relations
P.O. Box 719
Uhrichsville, OH 44683

ISBN 1-55748-872-X

GARMENT OF PRAISE

Cover illustration by Kay Salem.

PRINTED IN THE U.S.A.

one

Pulling the towel off her long auburn curls, Hailey wrinkled her nose at her blurred reflection in the bathroom mirror. Her finger squeaked on the glass as she drew a grinning smiley-face in the steam, then added glasses as an after-thought.

Poking her head out of the shower, her sister Karlee raised one eyebrow. "What are you doing?"

"Practicing for my interview." Hailey nodded to the man in the mirror. "This is Robert."

Karlee shook her head and closed the shower curtain. "Right."

Extending her hand, Hailey gave a firm handshake to the water faucet. "Hello, Dr. Worth. How are you on this beautiful spring morning? . . .Oh, please, call me Hailey. 'Miss Austin' is so formal." Her wide green eyes winked at the "doctor." "This old thing? Why, thank you, Doctor."

Karlee sputtered from behind the curtain. "Quit flirting! Robert's old enough to be your grandfather!"

"Ignore her, Doctor. . . .Of course, let's talk business. Why, Dr. Worth, I'm honored! You say my references were excellent? Superlative? Well, I just do my duty. Maybe I *am* a workaholic. . ."

Karlee stuck her head out and rolled her eyes. "She doesn't even make her own *bed*, Robert!"

"What was that again, Doctor? I'm not only talented and competent, I'm also beautiful? Why, Doctor. . . !"

There was a loud groan from the shower. "Tell her the truth, Robert!" Karlee yelled. "Tell her you're only offering her a job because her sister's future husband is the money and brains behind the Sparrow Center!"

Lifting her chin in mock disdain, Hailey chastised her sister, "Who invited you, anyway? And can't you take a *cold* shower? I'm losing Robert and it's all because of you!" She turned back to the disappearing face on the mist-coated mirror. "Dr. Worth! Dr. Worth! Come back to me!"

Karlee taunted, "Serves you right. I told you he was too old for you!" Turning off the water, she reached for the towel on the bar next to the shower, and then for the robe that hung beside it, but her hand found an empty hook. "Rrrr! You're wearing my robe again!"

"How can you tell?" Hailey asked innocently. "They're identical!"

"Because *mine* was on the hook when I went to bed last night and *yours* is in the wash!" Karlee's hand slipped out again and grabbed a bath sheet from the shelf. She wrapped it around herself, then stomped out of the bathroom. Slamming the door behind her, she muttered, "You'll pay for this, little sister!"

Hailey worked carefully through her tangled, waist-length hair with a wide comb, then scrunched the curls into shape with her fingers. After pulling her make-up bag from the drawer, she swiped a towel across the steam-fogged mirror, only to watch her image blur again. Knotting the tie of Karlee's peach robe tighter around her waist, she yanked the bathroom door open. The blast of cool air hit her face only a split second before the edge of the door slammed into her cheekbone. Reeling, Hailey grabbed the sink with one hand while her other flew to the stinging bump just below her right eye. Through the pain and shock, she was dimly aware of Karlee's gasp, followed by a torrent of incoherent sounds.

"I was just opening the. . .I didn't know you were . . . Are you all right?. . .I'm sorry!"

Tears welled uncontrollably in Hailey's eyes as her sister's hands guided her to sit on the edge of the bathtub. Karlee kneeled on the damp mat next to Hailey, still babbling. "Does it. . .ooh. . .it looks. . .ice—I'll get ice!"

In the sudden silence of Karlee's departure, Hailey listened to her niece and nephew giggling down in the kitchen, heard the freezer door slam, then recognized Karlee's footsteps flying up the stairs. Grabbing a hand mirror off the back of the toilet, Hailey groaned, "Why today?"

The ice pack sent needles down the side of her face and neck. She held it in place, her eyes shut, for several minutes before looking up to see Karlee's worried expression on the verge of crumpling. "I'm okay, Kar."

Karlee's bottom lip quivered. "I'm really sorry. I feel terrible! Here you have your interview this morning and you were nervous anyway, and now you have to go in with a black eye, and it's all my fault, and. . ."

The ice pack slapped gently over Karlee's mouth, stopping the flow of words. Hailey smiled, slightly lopsided. "David's right. You talk too much." Karlee cringed and Hailey gave an exaggerated groan. "I'm sorry! How could I have been so thoughtless! I uttered his precious name before the mail arrived!"

"It's not funny. Do you know how long it's been since I got a letter?"

Hailey threw her arm over her forehead. "Alas, the head-hunters finally got him." Her eyes sparkled wickedly as she painfully raised one eyebrow. "Or maybe he was swept off his feet by a dark-eyed African beauty. Don't they speak French in Senegal? The language of love. . ."

"It's been eleven days!"

"And eighteen hours and thirty-seven minutes and. . ." Fighting laughter, Karlee held up a fist in front of her sister's face. "I oughta' smack you again!"

Standing in front of the sink, Hailey looked in the mirror, prodding the purpling bump tenderly. "I really think once is sufficient."

"I could make both sides match!"

Hailey smiled, then winced as her cheek stretched. "Actually, it ought to go with my silk blouse perfectly!"

Karlee leaned in to take a closer look. "You're right! And that is your color!" She reached out and touched Hailey's cheek gently. "You'll thank me for this some day."

Raising both eyebrows, Hailey said, "And just when would that be?"

"When Robert hires you as Director of Nursing for the Sparrow Center."

"A black eye is going to land me an administrative position?"

"Guaranteed. He's a sucker for hard luck cases. You could really capitalize on this, you know. He may look strong, but he's nothing but mush on the inside."

"So's your head."

Karlee rolled her eyes. "Are you done in here?"

"Temporarily. What's your rush? It's early."

"I promised Mrs. Spellman that I'd help her piece her crazy quilt before my first class."

"An appropriate choice for Mrs. Spellman!"

Karlee sputtered, "*Hailey*!"

"Sorry. You have the patience of Job, sister, but. . . that's why you quilt and I don't."

"You just prefer sticking needles in something that *bleeds*!"

Hailey rolled her eyes. "I'm outa' here."

To her back Karlee called, "Bring my robe back!"

"Wash mine first!" Hailey almost tripped over Penny, the golden retriever, and Mrs. Patches, Karlee's aging calico cat, who were curled up together outside the bathroom door, waiting for their mistress. Before she caught her balance, she had a moment to envision herself showing up for her job interview with plaster casts and crutches to complement the black eye. "This is a dangerous house," she mumbled to the animals.

As she approached the top of the stairs, a streak of red caught her eye, and she paused to watch a cardinal on the limb of the tree that touched the arched window above the front door. The leaves of the maple were small and shiny; in January when she had moved in, the branches had been bare. She had no second thoughts about the changes the past five months had brought, although she sometimes questioned her own motives for leaving Nebraska. She had not been totally selfless when she had moved in with her sister and her children after the death of Karlee's husband, Brad.

T.J.'s angry voice disrupted her reflections. "I had it first!"

"So! It's not for boys, anyway!" Shelly cried.

Hailey smiled as she stepped into the room. She was used to the frequent squabbles between her nine-year-old nephew and his six-year-old sister, though it was unusual that they would be playing in her bedroom. "All right, you two little. . ." Her heart skipped. "Put that down! Right now! Shelly, give it to me! What were you doing in here, anyway?"

Tears welled in Shelly's eyes as she held out the small silver box. "I'm sorry," she whispered.

Hailey felt Karlee's hand on her shoulder. "What happened? T.J., what did you do?"

"We were just winding Aunt Hailey's music box. I didn't think. . ."

"Go downstairs. We'll talk about it when I get down there." The two filed silently past. "Did they break anything?" Karlee asked.

"No," Hailey answered weakly. Karlee stared at her sister's pale face. "They shouldn't have been in here. I'm sorry, Hailey."

Hailey shook her head, then stared down at the music box in her hand. "I've never yelled at them before. I shouldn't have. . ."

"You're just nervous. I'll keep them downstairs while you get ready." Giving her sister a hug, Karlee was surprised to feel her trembling in her arms.

two

Hailey gripped the brass handle, but dropped her hand before opening the tall front door of the Sparrow Children's Center.

The blossoming crab apple sapling behind her was reflected in the tinted glass of the door, and the air was sweet with its fragrance. Gathering her courage, she tried to peer inside. Plaster dust and strips of masking tape blocked her view, giving her only another glimpse of the image she had checked and re-checked in her bedroom mirror. She took off her soft-brimmed hat and straightened the already-straight paisley ribbon at the crown, then replaced the hat, squashing it low over her right eye, hoping its shadow and the layered wisps of hair that played along her cheekbone would camouflage what her make-up had failed to hide.

She brushed imaginary dust from the sleeve of her silk blouse, then tugged at the loose-fitting, heather-blue sweater that came almost to her knees. She kicked out one booted foot, sending ripples around the broomstick skirt that was swirled with streaks of blue and purple. Whispering a quick prayer, she reached for the door again.

As she tugged on the handle, the door flung out toward her with such speed that she gasped. Before she blinked, she had a fleeting sensation of déjà vu as something flew at her face.

"Whoa! Sorry!" She looked up in the direction of the deep voice, into the dark, paint-streaked face of a man at least a foot taller than her five foot three inches. He wore a faded blue flannel shirt and spattered jeans, and his black hair just touched the collar of his shirt in back. In front, it spilled recklessly over the twisted red bandanna tied across his forehead. Almost-black eyes and high, prominent cheekbones suggested a Native American heritage.

The man continued to apologize, the amusement in his voice defying the sincerity of his words. "I just thought I'd give you a hand with the door. It looked like you were having trouble opening it. I'm sorry."

Taking a shaky breath, Hailey stepped beneath the paintbrush in the hand that held the door open. The little confidence she had mustered was left on the other side of the door, and the irritating laughter of the man that towered over her did nothing to restore it. She felt her cheeks burn as her indignation grew, and she hurried to get past him.

"You're sure you're okay?"

"I'm fine!" she snapped. Straight ahead of her, she saw a wide front desk cluttered with boxes, and she stepped determinedly toward it.

"Wait! Uh. . .miss? Just a minute." There was still laughter in the deep voice. Hailey clenched her jaw and turned on her heel to face him, her hands in fists at her sides.

"You're, uh. . .not *quite* fine." From his back pocket he pulled a second red bandanna. "You've got a little. . .spot of paint." His hand moved toward her nose, then stopped.

Placing the bandanna in her hand, he repeated, "I'm really sorry. The ladies' room is over there; I hope the mirrors are up."

Hailey's short "thank you" hissed through tight lips as she hurried away, clutching the bandanna.

Scooping up a drink of cold water with her hand, Hailey leaned heavily on the sink. Her hands were shaking. She tried to tell herself that there was no reason for anxiety about the upcoming interview. With her resume, references, and ties to David Stern, senior architect and founder of the Sparrow Center and Karlee's fiancé, she was almost assured a job when the center opened in two months. There would be little competition for the six nursing positions available, as the non-profit organization could not compete with local wages.

As Hailey steadied her hand to touch up the concealer that she had wiped from her face along with the splotch of paint, it occurred to her, not for the first time, that she could simply walk away. She had a secure position working three to eleven at a private nursing home. The hours were not ideal, but that would change. The job offered little excitement, and the pay was much lower than she was used to, but the benefits were good. Besides, she reasoned, after three years in the neo-natal intensive care unit and a year on the cardiac wing, she had earned a break from the stress of constant emergencies.

But after several minutes spent trying to justify a retreat, Hailey walked out of the rest room and straight to the front desk. There was no excuse convincing enough, even to her own ears, and no way she could explain a change of mind to Karlee or David without raising questions she did not want to answer.

She picked up the watch pendant that hung around her neck. It was exactly nine o'clock. A wide hallway extended behind the desk with closed doors on each side. Hailey had seen enough of David's blueprints to know that these were offices, but she had no idea which one was Robert's, and, although she could hear the sound of power tools in the background, no one else appeared to be in the front of the building except the painter. He was singing to himself as he worked, and the tune echoed across the empty reception area.

Hailey drew circles in the dust-coated counter top and picked up her watch again. Finally, wiping her clammy palms on her sweater, she walked over to the front door.

She forced politeness into her tone. "Excuse me. . ."

He turned to face her and smiled. "Oh, hi! You look much . . .*cleaner*!" he said.

Hailey bit the tip of her tongue and sighed loudly. She was in no mood for this man's sense of humor. She'd met one too many smooth talkers in work boots. "Can you tell me where Dr. Worth's office is?"

"Uh. . .sure." He stood and reached for his back pocket. "I. . .uh, left your bandanna in the. . ."

"No problem," he said, wiping his hands on his hips and giving her a patronizing smile. "Dr. Worth's office is the first one on the right behind the desk. He's. . .um, not in yet, but go on in and wait."

Hailey was taken back by the hint of sarcasm in his last word. "Thank you," she clipped.

The office was nearly bare. Two chairs, a desk that held only a telephone, and a plastic milk crate filled with file folders took up the far wall beneath a tall, narrow window.

Hailey brushed off the chair facing the window and sat down. As she tapped her foot on the concrete floor, the sound bounced from wall to wall, jangling her nerves.

After the fifth time she'd looked at her watch, she heard a noise outside the open door and turned as the painter clattered into the room carrying three two-by-fours and several empty paint cans.

Hailey turned away quickly, stared down at her boots, then up at the window, waiting for him to leave. She kept her back to him as he leaned the boards against the door jam and set the paint cans down one at a time. The tiny hairs at the base of Hailey's neck stood out as silence swelled in the room and she felt his eyes on the back of her head.

Slowly, she turned slightly, just enough to see him standing by the door, hands on hips, grinning at her. Hailey raised her chin and arched her left brow. "Can I help you?"

"Well, yes, you can. Do you take cream or sugar?"

"*Excuse me?*"

"In your coffee. . .a little sugar might help."

Her temples were beginning to throb in unison with the lump on her cheek. "Have you seen Dr. Worth?" she demanded. "Is he here, in the building?" More quietly she added, "I can come back some—"

"No! I'll go get him. He's. . .in a phone booth. How did you say you liked your coffee?"

"I didn't," she snapped.

His smile was even more patronizing than before. "Then I'll just sweeten it a bit."

੨ゐ

Hailey took a tight breath and waited for the hot blush creeping up her neck to recede. Her forehead wrinkled as she whispered, "*Phone booth?*"

The second hand swept the face of her watch a full seven times before the painter returned, carrying two styrofoam cups. He set them down on the desk without a word, then stooped to pull a file from the milk crate near her feet. It was only then that Hailey noticed that he had changed into a dark blue denim shirt and white jeans, and he had removed the bandanna. He laid the file on the desk, pulled out the chair behind it, then leaned across the desk, extending his right hand to her.

"Miss Austin, I'm Dr. Worth. I'm very glad to meet you."

Hailey's head spun in confusion. "No, you're not!"

"Oh, I assure you, I'm very glad to meet you!"

"No! You're not Dr. Worth!"

The smile that spread across his dark face was warm and sincere. "My name's Dakota Wingreen Worth, but everyone calls me Cody. I'm Robert's son, a doctor of law, not medicine."

"Oh. *Oh.* . . ! I thought. . ."

He smiled. "I've only held the title for two weeks, but I can't imagine I'll ever enjoy it as much as I have the past few minutes!" He stopped to let his words have the desired effect on her. "I'm just helping out on the administrative end for a few months. Dad got called out on an emergency and I thought his secretary was going to call you from the hospital, but I've been helping with the interviewing anyway. . ."

The look of shock was fixed on her face. Cody's laugh was rich and deep as he stepped closer to her, around the corner of the desk. "Miss Austin, I don't know if it's painters you have a problem with, or Indians, but. . ."

Hailey gasped. "No! It's. . .neither!" she stammered, blinking fiercely at the tears that stung her eyes. "It's interviews I have a problem with, and doors in my face, and. . ."

She was stopped by his hand on her shoulder. "Have you had breakfast yet?"

Startled, she shook her head.

"I've been here since six-thirty and I'm starving." He picked up the file. "Could we conduct this interview over some waffles and *real* coffee?"

Hailey swiped at a stray tear and nodded, not trusting her voice. Once again, he extended his hand. "Can we start over?"

Nodding again, Hailey smiled weakly. He took her hand in his and shook it firmly. "Hailey Austin, I'm Cody Worth. And I *am* pleased to meet you."

three

Swallowing his last bite of blueberry waffle, Cody pushed aside his empty plate, took a sip of coffee, and closed the file folder that had lain open beside him on the table.

Hailey breathed a small sigh, letting a little of the tension slip from her shoulders. The interview hadn't been as nerve-wracking as she'd feared. She smiled across the table. "I really am sorry I acted like such a snob this morning."

"Forget it. If my day had started with a door, make that *two*, in my face, I'd have been a bit testy, too. And I'll take part of the blame—from the moment you walked past me with your nose in the air I had you pegged as just another yuppy bigot."

"Strong words."

"I've locked horns with a lot of them over the past few years—it's turned me a bit cynical."

"What changed your mind about me?"

Cody returned her smile, but with a hint of shyness that disarmed her. "Promise you won't be embarrassed?" he asked.

"No, I can't promise that. But tell me anyway."

"It was that one little tear rolling down over your purple cheek."

Hailey blushed and instinctively covered her cheek.

His chin rested on his hands, and without shifting his position, he pointed one index finger at her. "That's the look. I'm a pretty good judge of faces—you were so flustered, I knew I'd misjudged you."

A comfortable silence followed. Hailey sipped her coffee, sizing up the man across from her over the rim of her cup.

"Phone booth!" she almost shouted, surprising even herself. "I get it!" She laughed, as much at the look on Cody's face as at the joke itself.

"Very good. Not real quick. . .but good."

Trying not to acknowledge the effect his smile was having on her, she reminded herself that every Superman had a Clark Kent side. But the "before" picture of the paint-spattered jeans and red bandanna that flashed in her mind did little to diminish her interest.

Cody laid a tip on the table, then tapped his fingers on the file folder. "Can I be blunt, Hailey?" he asked softly.

She tried a confident smile, but failed. "I doubt that I could stop you."

"This just doesn't make any sense to me. I'm a lawyer, not a medical doctor, and I'm trained to look at things with pure logic—maybe there's something here that will make more sense to my dad. . ." He took off the small, round, wire-rimmed glasses he had put on to read her resume. "You're certainly *qualified* for either the director of nursing position or the occupational therapy position, and I'm sure you'd do an excellent job in either one, but. . ." He folded his hands in front of him and leaned toward her. Hailey squirmed under his intense dark gaze.

"You're applying for a job at a facility that's sole purpose is to treat and care for children with Fetal Alcohol Syndrome and drug-related disorders. You've had three years experience in a neo-natal intensive care unit with hands-on experience with crack and FAS babies, plus numerous seminars on the subject. . ." He took a deep breath and another sip of coffee before continuing. "Add to all this the fact that the position we're most concerned about filling is that of head nurse in the intensive care nursery, and," hc clenched a fist and tapped it on the file for emphasis, "and you won't even *consider* the position?"

Hailey picked at the fruit on her plate, looked up at the man across from her, then quickly lowered her eyes, searching for a plausible excuse. "I don't think I was ever cut out for the pressure, the emergencies. . .I think I'd do much better in personnel, or working with. . .older. . .residents."

Cody's eyes narrowed as he smiled. "Believe me, stress is something I understand. Why do you think I'm spending the summer volunteering at the Sparrow Center just after completing my doctorate? I can certainly relate to your need for a break, but. . ."

He stopped in mid-sentence and Hailey had the feeling he was afraid to go on. Hesitantly, she asked, "But what?"

Cody stared into his coffee cup, then looked up at her, searching her face. "But it just docsn't make sense. Look, I'm not trying to push you into something you're not comfortable with. I know you said you've only been a Christian for a few months, and sometimes it's hard to discern what God wants. . . but, on the surface," he smiled slightly, "*logically*, you seem to be the perfect person for head nurse in the intensive care nursery. It looks to me like 'Direction' with a capital 'D'!"

Nervously, Hailey cleared her throat. "I don't know. Could I have some time. . .to pray about this? I'm just. . ."

Cody held his hand up to stop her. "No pressure. Really. We'll keep the ad listed. Actually, there have been more applications than expected, but Dad's had it in his head that you were the one for the job." He grinned sheepishly and shrugged. "This interview was supposed to be just a chance to let you ask questions and get to know you better."

Hailey grimaced and Cody shook his head. "I'm sorry. I promised 'no pressure,' didn't I?"

"Could we just change the subject for a while?" She met his eyes briefly again. "Besides, it's my turn to ask questions."

Leaning back in the booth, Cody smiled. "That's fair. Shoot."

"Okay. Obvious questions first. Were you adopted?"

Cody's eyes widened and he straightened in his seat. Hailey wrinkled her nose. "Was that tacky?"

"No!" he laughed. "That was *wonderful*! Most people dance around in circles to avoid the word!"

"I've been told that I have a straightforward approach to things." She smiled. "Actually, I've been told that I'm basically rude."

"You have no idea how refreshing you are, Hailey. Ever since my dad adopted me, people have tried to pretend they don't even notice I don't exactly look like my father. I went through phases as a kid where even I tried to pretend I just had a great tan, but Dad has always set me straight. He worked hard at making me proud of my heritage."

"Were you adopted at birth?"

"No. I was nine. Actually, Robert is my step-father, but it's a long story." Hailey looked at him expectantly. "Do you really want to hear it?" he asked.

"Yes."

"Okay. I need to stop home and pick up some papers. Do you have time to ride along?"

"I don't have to work until one."

Cody picked up the check and smiled. "Great."

❧

Without prompting, Cody began his story as he turned the car onto the highway. "My mother died when I was nine, but the story really starts before that. My parents met at a mission church near Missoula, Montana. My father was in the Jesus People movement—VW bus and everything. He was with a group that traveled around the country singing and preaching. He led my mother to the Lord and then fell in love with her and stayed behind when the rest of the group left.

"It would have been a perfect love story, except that my grandparents hated him. He was white and a Christian, not a good combination in their eyes; they were irate when she married him. Three months later my father was drafted. A month after he was sent to Vietnam, my mother found out she was expecting me, but before she could write him with the news, she got word that he had been shot down. The pilot who had witnessed it said there couldn't have been any survivors, but I'm not sure my mother ever quite let herself believe it.

"I had a pretty normal, happy childhood until I was eight. Then my mother moved us to Edgewater to get away from her family. She worked at an art gallery and we lived above the shop. The owners were like grandparents to me." Cody turned the car onto a narrow country road and was silent for several minutes.

"Anyway, we first met Robert when I was five. He spent a couple weeks every summer volunteering at a free clinic near us. The first year he was there I was in the hospital for a week with pneumonia, then two years later I fell off my bike and broke my collar bone—I guess I was responsible for bringing them together. They spent a lot of time together while he was in Montana and wrote to each other when he was back here." Cody put on his turn signal and glanced at Hailey. "Still with me?"

"Yes!"

He pulled into a winding drive that led to a nineteenth-century, two-story white house with a wide porch and second-story balcony. "This is Dad's place, mine's in back. Want to come in for a minute?"

Without her usual caution, Hailey followed him up the cobblestone walkway.

"This used to be the summer house. The main house was built by Milbrooke's first mayor, and this was added during the twenties." He opened the door for her.

The living room of the low-ceilinged bungalow was newly carpeted in a light teal, with matching vertical blinds on the windows. An arched fireplace was tiled in terra cotta; the stark white walls were accented by several Southwest prints. It was a peaceful place, Hailey thought.

"I'll grab the papers, make yourself at home for a minute," Cody said.

Hailey's eyes were drawn to the painting that hung above the fireplace. The room seemed to have been decorated around its color scheme. Hailey touched the smooth, blonde wood of the frame and stared at the scene above her. A row of small clapboard store fronts, shaded by a covered boardwalk, was nestled at the foot of a cloud-covered mountain. Streaks of sunlight filtered through the clouds and dappled the dirt street in front of the buildings. Such a common scene, yet it held an almost ethereal quality.

"Like it?" Cody asked.

She nodded.

"It's one of my mother's."

Hailey shook her head sadly. "She was very gifted." She turned to a smaller painting. "Did she do this one, too?"

"No. There are only two; Dad has the other one."

"You know Paige, David's sister, I suppose."

"I just met her yesterday. Studied art in Paris, huh?"

"Yes. She's going back in the fall. She just started working for a gallery in Madison. You should see her work."

She was about to comment that he and Paige had a lot in common, but something stopped her. She walked quietly to a narrow table that was crowded with picture frames and picked up the one in the Center. A woman with long black hair, wearing a traditional Indian dress of white buckskin, trimmed with beads and layers of fringe, stood beside a man with a dark beard and hair to his shoulders. A brass plaque on the frame read, "Richard and Kwanita." Almost in awe, Hailey whispered, "Your parents?"

"Mm-hm. Their wedding picture."

"Your mother was beautiful." She was about to set it down, then pulled it closer, turning it so that the light from the window illuminated the beaded headband that held the long, black hair in place. "I've seen. . ." she hesitated. "What?"

Hailey shook her head again. "Oh. . .nothing."

She set the frame down and focused on the picture next to it. A dark-haired little boy sat between a gray-haired couple; behind them stood a stern-faced man in his thirties, with cold, piercing eyes. She pointed to the child. "Is that you?"

"Yeah. Cute wasn't I? That's Pampa and Millie Waters, the shop owners I told you about." His voice altered slightly as he pointed to the younger man in the picture. "That's their nephew, Lyle, a real deadbeat. Used to show up whenever he needed money. He was always after my mother; I remember being terrified of him when I was little. He's the reason things weren't so happy for me after we moved when I was eight."

Cody straightened the stack of file folders in his hand. "Ready to go? I'll finish my life story on the way back."

Hailey nodded and turned to follow him, then glanced back, puzzled, at the wedding picture. She opened her mouth in a silent question, then stepped beneath his arm and out the door.

four

The night air was warm and fresh, and although the car's digital clock read 9:22 as Hailey pulled into the driveway, she was revived by the knowledge that she had the next day off. She locked her black Blazer, then threw her keys into the bottom of her leather bag.

As she stepped into the darkened kitchen, the low, humming sound and the soft light coming from the living room warned her what she was in for. She untied her white shoes and slipped them off by the door, then padded silently into the room where Karlee was curled on the couch. Hailey tossed her suede jacket on the arm, only to watch it slide to the floor.

Meeting Karlee's eyes with a defiant smile that dared her to ask her to pick it up, she stepped over the jacket and plopped onto the couch, clapping her hands together in a child-like gesture. "Oh, goody! By my educated estimation, this viewing of 'Slides from Senegal' must be about number eleven hundred and thirty-four. So, are we in love today, or is this a pity-party?"

Karlee faced her sister, her face expressionless. "I think a little respect is in order. You are sitting on *my* couch, littering up *my* living room, and interrupting *my* pity-party! But, for your information, these are new slides." She pointed to the tip of a padded brown envelope that peeked out from beneath the quilt that covered her.

Karlee rolled her eyes and flipped to another slide, a

picture of David in shorts and a T-shirt, standing on a ladder. She sighed longingly and Hailey followed with a perfect imitation.

"You live to irritate me, don't you?"

Hailey nodded. "Always have."

"What are you doing home so early, anyway?" Karlee straightened and leaned toward Hailey. "Did 'someone' quit after being hired at the Sparrow Center this morning?"

"No. 'Someone' had to go in early today so I got off earlier. I guess I forgot to tell you."

"Well. . .how did the interview go? Was Robert reduced to mush over your black eye?"

Hailey stood and took a step toward the stairs. "Are the kids asleep? I brought them something."

"You don't have to buy them stuff all the time! You're making me look bad! Besides, you want them to feel deprived after we move and Aunt Hailey isn't there to shower them with goodies?"

"You'll only be a few miles away. Who says it has to stop?" She ducked as a pillow flew past her head. "I . . .kinda figured I owed them something after this morning."

"They know they're not supposed to play in your room. They needed to be scolded."

"Not like. . ." She turned and took another step toward the stairs, pulling two rolls of candy out of her uniform pocket.

"I'll just leave these on their dressers." She stopped and faced Karlee, the teasing gone from her voice. "How *is* David? Everything going okay with the building?"

Karlee nodded. "Their part is almost done—the local

people can do the finishing work. They held their first church service in the school building." Hesitantly she added, "Would you like to see the slides?"

"Oh, I'd hate to make you go through them again just for me." Karlee wrinkled her nose and Hailey laughed. "Okay, I'll be your excuse to look at them another time, after I get out of this uniform—*if* you make popcorn."

"That sounds like blackmail."

"It is. Extra butter, please."

"At eleven grams of fat per tablespoon?"

"Who cares? I'll have a diet soda." She took two more steps toward the stairs before Karlee's voice stopped her.

"Hey! Did Robert give you the job or not?"

Without turning around, Hailey said, "He wasn't there," and walked up the stairs.

*

Hailey entered the kitchen wrapped in Karlee's peach robe. As she reached into the popcorn bowl, Karlee touched her bruised cheek. "You look awful."

"Thank you. More butter."

"You're depressed. You eat when you're depressed."

"I'm hungry. I eat when I'm hungry."

"Right. Oh, there's a message on the answering machine for you."

"Really? Who?"

"Such interest! Who were you expecting? It was just Paige. Something about lunch tomorrow and painting at the Center."

"Oh. I ran into her after my interview. She wants help with her murals." The blush creeping up her cheeks startled her, and she turned away from Karlee and grabbed the salt shaker. "She asked me to help."

"Wait a minute. You had your interview? You said Robert wasn't there."

Hailey grabbed the bowl and headed for the living room. "He wasn't."

When they were settled on the couch with the quilt over their knees and the popcorn bowl between them, Hailey tried to conjure a nonchalant attitude as she waited for the inevitable.

"Do I have to play twenty questions?" Karlee asked.

"About what?"

"Okay. I'll play along. Just answer 'yes' or 'no'. Did you have an interview today?"

"Yes."

"Did you see Dr. Worth today?"

"Yes."

"Did you see him at the Sparrow Center?"

"Yes."

"But you said. . .did Robert interview you somewhere else today?"

"No."

"So you had your interview at the Sparrow Center?"

"No."

"Aaaaah!" Karlee threw a handful of popcorn at her sister. "You drive me crazy!"

"Mutual, I'm sure," Hailey teased in a nasal twang, emphasized by a return barrage of popcorn.

The popcorn flew for several minutes until Karlee could stop laughing long enough to yell. "*Your* 'extra butter' is going to stain *my couch!*"

Hailey put on a repentant face and began picking popcorn off the floor and out of her hair, then sat down again. "Okay, let's drool over David."

Karlee slapped her playfully on top of her head. "If I didn't know you so well I'd think you were trying to change the subject."

"Who me? Never. I really want to see these pictures."

Karlee turned on the slide projector, then began her narrative on the progress of the school that David and a group of missionary students had designed and almost completed. Hailey grew serious, asking questions and listening intently.

"He really is wonderful, Kar."

Karlee nodded. "I still can't believe this incredible man has asked me to marry him. A year ago my whole world caved in and now it's starting over."

"Kar, do you still miss Brad?" It had been weeks since they had had a deep discussion and Hailey approached the subject gently.

Karlee's smile was sweet. "Sure. I suppose I always will, but God has given me something so precious. . ."

They were silent for several minutes, then Hailey said softly, "I memorized your verse." She fixed her eyes on David's broad smile. Isaiah 61:3 was the verse that had pulled him out of depression after his wife's death in the country where he now served. David had shared it with Karlee, and now Hailey tried to draw comfort from the words.

Quietly, she quoted the verse. "'To appoint unto them that mourn in Zion, to give unto them beauty for ashes, the oil of joy for mourning, the garment of praise for the spirit of heaviness; that they might be called trees of righteousness, the planting of the Lord, that he might be glorified.'"

Karlee put her arms around her. "Have I told you lately that I love you, little sister?"

Hailey rested her head on Karlee's shoulder, and they

turned back to the screen. After three more slides, Hailey said quietly, "I want a David."

Karlee patted her shoulder. "You'll get one. I'm praying for him, whoever he is."

After several more minutes, Hailey asked casually, "Have you ever met Robert's son Cody?"

"No. I've heard about him, of course. In fact, David asked about him in his letter. Said he just got his doctorate in law and is planning on spending the summer. . .*wait a minute*! That would make him Dr. Worth, right?"

"I suppose."

"You little. . .*he* interviewed you!"

"Uh-huh."

"And obviously left a good impression."

"Maybe. Not that it matters, I made a *horrible* first impression on him!" She covered her face with her hands and moaned, "Oh, Kar, I made a perfect spectacle of myself!"

"Don't be so melodramatic. Even *you* couldn't have been that bad!"

"You're right—I was worse!" As she retold the events of the morning, Karlee convulsed in laughter. Her comforting words were anything but convincing.

"Well, if Cody is anything like Robert, I'm sure he has discernment and wisdom."

"Then he should be wise enough not to hire me!"

"*Did* he hire you?"

"Yes, in a way, I mean Robert had. . .already, sort of. I said I wanted to think about it." Quickly she headed off more questions. "Do you know about Cody? Did you know he's Robert's stepson?"

"I knew that, but that's about all."

"Oh, Kar, it's such a beautiful, sad story! His mother

found out she had leukemia when he was only eight and Robert married her two months before she died so that her parents couldn't have any claim on Cody. They were close friends before that, but they really fell in love those last few weeks. And to hear him tell it. . .he was so little . . ." Hailey sighed and sat back on the couch, closing her eyes and hugging a pillow close to her, aware that Karlee was staring at her intently. She was almost asleep when a disturbing thought pricked her consciousness.

"Hey, Kar, remember that painting at Paige's gallery?"

"Which one?"

"Oh, never mind." She yawned dreamily. "I just . . .liked it."

five

"Hey, Kar?" Hailey yelled up the stairs. "Paige is on the phone. She says you're supposed to come with us for lunch and then help paint afterwards. She says you should call Jody and ask her to keep the kids."

Karlee came to the top of the stairs with a basket of laundry. Laughing, she said, "Does she also say what I should wear and what I should order for lunch?"

"I'll ask." She ran to the kitchen, then ran back, meeting Karlee in the dining room. "She said you should wear your best sweats and eat French onion soup!"

Rolling her eyes, Karlee said, "I suppose she's going to video this for David!"

"I'll ask!" Giggling, Hailey turned on her heels and ran back to the kitchen.

Karlee yelled to her back. "Tell her 'yes' to everything but the soup! Tell her I'm saving my onion breath for her brother!"

❧

"Stay in the lines, you two!" Paige cried in mock exasperation, then glanced at her watch.

"Oh, lighten up," Hailey laughed, "you're stifling our creativity."

"I think I should stick to quilting," Karlee laughed. She looked over at the wavy edge of Hailey's thorn bush, "And you should stick to drawing blood!" The other two groaned loudly.

Paige had spent three days penciling in an African grass-land scene on two walls of the employee break room, and now the three of them were filling it in with color.

Paige turned to Hailey. "Did you make a decision on your job here yet?"

Hailey paused. "I've. . .decided to work here. I'll give my notice at the nursing home in a couple weeks."

"I eavesdropped on Robert and his son this morning, not on purpose, of course. They're set on you being in charge of the intensive care nursery, but you're still not sure, huh?" Waiting for an answer, Paige glanced at the door and then at her watch.

Hailey bent over her paint can, carefully dipping her brush into the brown paint. "Well, I. . ."

"Coffee, ladies?" Hailey's brush slipped at the sound of Cody's voice. He was carrying three styrofoam cups. Handing one to Paige, he said, "Black," then turned to Hailey. Holding out another cup, he winked and said, "Sweetened up a bit," and then turned to Karlee. "And you must be the future Mrs. Stern. Coffee?"

"No, thank you, I'm decaffeinated. Hailey will drink mine though—she's an addict." Holding out her paint-smeared hand to Cody, Karlee laughed, then hid it behind her back. "I'm Karlee Merrick. You must be *Dr*. Worth the second." She shot a smirking smile at Hailey, whose blush deepened.

"Call me Cody." He looked over the room and nodded. "I'm impressed. This was a great idea, Paige—it'll take away some of that 'institution' atmosphere—make it more homey. Well, I've got to get back to my paint can. Keep up the good work." He set the coffee cup on the step ladder and walked out.

Paige took a sip from her cup, then nodded toward the door. "You know, he's been here every morning before seven, and it's all voluntary. What a sweetheart."

Karlee glanced quickly at her sister, who was carefully cleaning the brush handle that had fallen into the paint can, then turned to Paige. "Sounds like more than a passing interest. No wonder you've been staring at your watch all afternoon!"

"I have?" Paige laughed nervously. "I only met him a few days ago. He's a bit too lawyer-ish for me, but he makes up for it in looks, doesn't he? Who knows?"

Hailey was startled by her own reaction to Paige's answer: a twinge that could only be labeled envy. Paige, with her short, glossy dark hair that swung over one eye and had to be brushed back constantly by long, artistic fingers; Paige, with her large blue-green eyes, quick smile and tiny, petite figure, all combined with a personality that seemed oblivious to all these gifts; Paige, to whom any man would be bound to be attracted.

Hailey chastised herself. Karlee had offered to rent her house to Paige and Hailey after she and David were married; this was not the attitude to have toward a future roommate. She took a deep breath and forced enthusiasm into her voice. "How are plans coming for the open house?"

"I just took the invitations to the printer yesterday," Paige swept out her hand in a motion that included the entire building, "so all of this had better get done on time!"

Karlee asked, "Are there doubts?"

"I guess I'm just worried about my part in this, but I think Robert and the Cedar Ridge contractors feel things are under control. As soon as the painting is done and the flooring down, it's just a matter of moving everything in.

Most of the equipment for the nurseries is already here, just waiting to be put in, and the kitchen is almost done. I'd like to get all the murals done before the carpeting goes in, but maybe that's a bit ambitious. How are the quilts coming, Karlee?"

"We've finished all the crib quilts and about half of the rest of them. I've got some real dedicated people working some long hours."

Since January, Karlee had gone back to teaching quilting classes at the woolen mill run by her best friend, Jody Hansen. Several of the classes had taken on the project of furnishing quilts for all of the cribs and beds in the Sparrow Center.

"I need some ideas for food. I'd planned on having the open house catered, but there really isn't any money for that."

"I'm sure we could ask the women's fellowship group at the church to make finger sandwiches or something," Karlee said. She smiled a little-girl smile. "Although I don't think *I'm* going to be much earthly good after David gets home."

Hailey shook her head and pointed to the blobs of bright green paint spattered across Karlee's faded pink sweatshirt. "I'm not sure you're much earthly good even now!"

Paige laughed, pulled her sleeve back away from her watch, then balanced her paint brush on the top of her can. "I'm going to go. . .find some more rags," she said.

She was back in ten minutes, grinning, looking flushed, and empty-handed. Hailey fought the rising green monster inside her as she heard Cody's laugh ring out from a muffled conversation in the hallway. "Couldn't find any rags?" she asked, with as little sarcasm as she could manage.

"Rags? Oh, no. . .we'll have to use paper towels, I guess."

She reached for the roll that was sitting on the ladder. "So, Karlee, what do you hear from my brother these days?"

A quick shift, Hailey thought.

"I got more slides yesterday. You'll have to come and see them."

"How long has he been gone now?"

Karlee bit her bottom lip as she concentrated on keeping her kelly green paint within the lines, but the answer didn't take concentration. "One hundred and twenty-three days, and at least fourteen more to go."

"Miss him quite a bit, don't you?"

Karlee sighed. "Uh-huh."

"Just what do you see in him, anyway?" Paige asked.

Karlee closed her eyes. "I see the kindest, most interesting, most Christ-like man I've ever known—and on top of that I see the most handsome man I've ever met in my life, with the bluest eyes, and the sweetest, tenderest smile, and the strongest arms, and. . ."

"And you'd see him a lot better if you'd open your eyes!"

Karlee gasped and whirled toward the deep, familiar voice. "David!" Tears filled her eyes, but she was frozen to the spot. Paige stepped over and took the brush from her hand as Hailey grabbed the paint can from the other. Together they gave her a gentle shove, and she was wrapped in David's arms, sobbing.

"Why? How? Why didn't. . .Paige knew! This isn't fair! I look so. . ."

David pulled away from her and covered her lips with his finger tips. "You look so beautiful, but you still talk too much!" Slowly, he lifted his fingers, one at a time, then covered her lips with his mouth Hailey and Paige sighed wistfully in unison, then tactfully left the room. Smiling through her tears, Karlee took a half step back to stare at him. "I'm getting paint all over you!" she cried.

Staring down at the finger-streaks of blue and green on his white shirt sleeves, David said, "You just added to the masterpiece Paige started earlier when she first saw me." He ran the back of his hand along her cheek, and Karlee watched his sapphire eyes fill with tears. Softly he whispered, "I've always loved you in green," and closed her in his arms again.

six

Hailey leaned against the front desk, her chin resting on her left arm. Next to her, Paige was her mirror image. The two followed David's every move and expression as Karlee led him into the reception area at the end of their tour through the Sparrow Center. Hailey sighed, as she had frequently during the hour since David had arrived on the scene. "They're so perfect together."

Paige nodded and wiped at a stray tear. "Can you imagine how he must feel? Here he designed every inch of this place on paper and then left before it was even started. . ."

They laughed together as David's hand went from caressing the oak trim around the front door to touching Karlee's face, then lifting her chin for a kiss.

"I think he's having a 'conflict of interests' problem!" Paige said.

Watching her sister's arms wrap around David's neck, Hailey smiled. "I don't think Karlee's having any trouble sorting out her priorities."

"Have you ever been that serious about anyone?" Paige asked.

Hailey shook her head. "I thought I was in love a few times in high school, but nothing for real, and nursing school isn't exactly the place to meet men—there were eight guys in my graduating class."

"How 'bout since then?"

Hailey was silent for a moment, then shrugged her

shoulders and said, "Nothing serious."

"Doesn't it bother you that you're twenty-seven and single?"

"Not like it did before I came here. It scares me to think what I might have ended up with before I became a believer. I mean, none of the guys I've dated could hold a candle to David."

Paige laughed. "According to your sister and my mother, God broke the mold after He made David. I think we have to lower our standards!" She turned toward Hailey. "Being single in Paris was wonderful. Not that I dated so much. . ." She made a face. "There are some really weird guys in the art community, and very few Christians, but I just enjoyed the freedom. Here it's different, things are more family-oriented or something." She nodded toward David and Karlee. "Watching those two doesn't help."

"You should join Edna's Bible study. We were talking about marriage last week. Anyway, I'm just going to wait on the Lord to bring the right guy into my—" Hailey jumped as a hand touched her shoulder.

"Mind if I join you, ladies, while you watch the show?" Cody laughed as David and Karlee pulled away from each other and caught the three of them staring in their direction. David shook his head and Karlee laughed. "I sold tickets," she said, wrinkling her nose at him.

Paige walked over to join them. Taking David's hand, she said, "Come on. I told Mom I'd make you call as soon as Karlee let go of you."

Watching them leave, Cody sighed, and Hailey wondered if the romance of the moment had gotten to him. However, she soon found his thoughts to be somewhat different from hers and Paige's.

"Can you imagine having enough money to be in full-time mission work without having to raise support?" he asked.

"Does that interest you, Doctor?"

"Just one of those 'impossible dreams,' I guess."

Hailey smiled up at him. "'O ye of little faith.'"

He returned her smile and shrugged. He was wearing white overalls over a navy thermal-underwear shirt that conformed to his muscular shoulders. This time a purple bandanna was tied around his head. He turned around and pulled himself up to sit on the counter. "Gotta get off my feet—it's been a long day."

Hailey felt awkward, standing beside his knee and craning her neck to look up at him. She took a half step away just as his hand reached out to her. Carefully, he lifted the strands of hair that had strayed out of her ponytail and stared down at her cheek. "Looks like the swelling's gone down some. Still hurt a lot?"

Hailey felt the heat from the fingertips that were not quite touching her face. It was enough to muddle her thoughts and his words took a moment to penetrate. "Only if I bend over," she finally answered. "It looks a lot worse than it feels."

"Oh, I don't know. . .I think it's kind of cute. It gives you character." Slowly, he let the wisps slip through his fingers and pulled his hand away.

Turning to hide the blush that was warming her cheeks, Hailey jumped up on the counter next to him. They sat in silence for a minute, staring down at the floor.

"You have small feet," he said, extending one long leg next to hers.

Hailey straightened her leg and laughed at the comparison.

For lack of a wittier remark, she was about to ask him what size shoe he wore, but Cody spoke first. "Have you ever done any public speaking?" he asked.

Hailey arched her left eyebrow and cocked her head to one side as she looked at him.

"Did I shift gears too fast?"

She smiled and nodded. "How did we get from my feet to my mouth? Must be one of those lawyer tricks to confuse the jury."

"I have a quick mind. What can I say? Looking at my boots reminded me that I have to figure out which box my good shoes are packed in because I promised Dad I'd talk to some civic group on Tuesday night, and that reminded me that he suggested I ask you to go along because you could talk about the medical aspects while I give some background on the Sparrow Center and beg for money."

Rolling her eyes, Hailey said, "Quick mind—long wind! Sounds like an Indian name, doesn't it?" She raised her hand. "How, Chief Quick Mind-Long Wind!"

Cody laughed and leaned briefly against her. "'How' to *you*, 'Little Foot-Big Mouth'! Don't you know Indian jokes are in very poor taste these days?"

With a repentant look, Hailey said, "Sorry, Chief, little foot stuck in big mouth again!"

Sliding off the counter, Cody turned to face her. He was grinning, and Hailey noticed for the first time the dimples shadowed by a two-day beard, and the cheek bones, high and strong, and—she thought of his parent's wedding picture—his mother's features. *That picture. . .*

"Well, Little Foot?"

Hailey blinked hard, trying to remember the question she was supposed to answer. Helplessly, she bit her bottom lip, then asked, "Well, what?"

Cody's brow furrowed slightly. "Do you have to work or can you come with me Tuesday night?"

"Oh, Tuesday. . .no. I mean, yes, I don't have to work!" It was several seconds before she remembered to what she was agreeing.

*

Later that afternoon, Hailey hung her paint clothes on a nail in what would eventually be a storeroom. She could hear Cody's rich tenor voice singing the chorus to "The Old Rugged Cross" as she stepped out of the room. Just then she spotted Paige walking down the hall.

"Psst! Paige, in here!" she whispered.

Paige looked at her quizzically as she back-tracked toward her. "What is it?"

"I've been wanting to ask you something."

"Okay. So ask."

"Have you ever been to Cody's house?"

"No," she answered suspiciously, "have you?"

"Well, yes, but. . ."

"Why are we whispering?" Paige interrupted.

Hailey bent her head in the direction of Cody's voice. "Cause I don't want him to hear. Remember that picture in your gallery, the one of the Indian woman with the blue headband?"

"Yeah. . .what about it?"

"Where did it come from—did you buy it, or are you selling it for someone?"

"It's on consignment." Paige thought a minute. "A woman, can't think of her name, she's a professor at the University. History, I think. . .She bought it for a specific spot in her condo, but it was too big."

"Where'd she get it?"

Paige's brow furrowed as she stared at Hailey. "New Mexico, I think. Yeah, New Mexico. She gave us a copy of a magazine article on Southwestern art that the painting was featured in. I hope you're not interested in it—I think we have a buyer."

"Oh no, you can't!" Compounding Paige's confusion, Hailey added, "There's something you have to see." She rubbed her temples, trying to devise a plan. Suddenly, a smile lit her face and she grabbed Paige by the arm. "C'mon, it's time to get domestic. Karlee has this awesome recipe for blueberry pie. . ."

&

Hailey shut off the car and switched off the headlights. No lights were on in the front of Cody's house, but a dim glow came from a side window near the back. They got out of the car and started up the cobblestone walk.

"He's probably in bed," Paige whispered. She handed the still-warm pie to Hailey.

"It's only 9:30. Besides, if you hadn't messed up the first two batches of pie crust we could have been here hours ago!"

"Me? What about. . . ?"

"Sh! He'll hear you!"

Paige bared her teeth and snarled at Hailey as they stepped up to the door. "Why am I doing this? This is crazy! Why don't you just say, 'Hey, Cody, did anybody ever paint a picture of your. . . ?'" She froze as the porch light came on and the front door opened.

Cody stood in the doorway in worn jeans with holes in the knees and a sleeveless sweatshirt. His feet were bare. He looked puzzled as he took off his wire-rimmed glasses and said, "Hi!"

Balancing the pie in her left hand, Hailey raised her right hand. "How, Chief, we bring pie!" She held it out to him, then pulled it back as he reached for it. She was dimly aware of the shocked expression on Paige's face as she kept talking.

"It's still hot. I'll just carry it into the kitchen." Cody backed out of the way, and she stepped in, followed slowly by a reluctant Paige.

Once inside, Hailey stopped in the entryway and signaled toward the living room with her eyes. Paige nodded almost imperceptibly, and Hailey turned her attention to Cody. "Lead the way, Chief," she said.

Cody flipped on the kitchen light and stood with his arms folded as Hailey set the pie on the table. "What did I do to deserve this?"

All of Hailey's rehearsed excuses fled. "Uh. . .well, blueberries are so cheap this time of year and, uh, Paige and I just love to bake, but—" she patted her hips, "we just can't risk the calories, you know!" She looked past him toward the living room, then pulled out a chair. "Why don't you just sit down and I'll cut you a piece." Aware that she was prattling, she made a conscious effort to slow her voice as Cody obediently took the chair. Her eyes swept the kitchen and stopped at the dish rack full of clean dishes. She pulled out a sharp knife, a fork, and a small plate.

She was just starting to cut into the pie when Paige popped into the room. Paige was slightly breathless as she said, "Well, Cody, I hope you enjoy your pie." She pointed to her watch and met Hailey's eyes with an intense stare, then flashed Cody a smile. "Hailey promised me I'd be in bed by ten tonight. Come on, Hailey, I just hate going to church with bags under my eyes." She grabbed Hailey's elbow, forcing her to set the knife down.

"Well, I guess you'll have to serve yourself, Chief. Good night."

Cody stood, a bewildered look on his face. "Good night, and. . .thanks, but why do I get the feeling you two are up to something?"

His question went unanswered.

Paige was halfway to the car by the time Hailey reached the front door. She turned one last time to face Cody. "Good night," she said.

Cody shook his head, still perplexed. "See you Tuesday, Little Foot."

❧

Hailey slid into the driver's seat and glared at Paige. "Bags under your eyes? What's going on? What's the rush?"

Paige looked ready to burst. "You were wrong about the painting. I mean, you were right, sort of, but you were wrong, too."

"Ahh! You're talking like me! Make sense, girl!"

"Didn't you tell me that Cody said there were only two paintings done by his mother?"

Hailey nodded and Paige took a deep breath. "I studied the wedding picture and the painting above the fireplace, the strokes, and style and everything, and I don't think the one in the gallery is a painting someone did of Cody's mother. I mean I think it *is* his mother, but I think, I'm not positive, I'll have to compare the signature, but I *think* the painting at the gallery is a *self*-portrait." At Hailey's sharp intake of breath she elaborated, "I think it was painted *by* his mother!"

seven

"You're sure you don't mind leaving early?" Hailey asked.

Her palm felt damp against the telephone receiver and she tapped her foot anxiously.

"No, it sounds like fun," Cody answered. "In fact, why don't we leave early enough so we can stop for dinner after the gallery?"

"Okay. I'll be at an in-service until about 2:30—that's the only reason I'm not working tomorrow night—so we could leave any time after three."

"Then I'll pick you up at 3:30 if that's okay. That'll get us to Madison a little after four. The meeting doesn't start until 7:30 so we should have plenty of time for everything."

"I'll be ready."

&

Cody opened the car door and Hailey slid in. Before closing the door, he bent down and said, "You look very nice."

She smoothed her skirt, then fingered the gold buttons on the cuffs of her sleeves. She wore hunter green suede heels that picked up the color in the dark print of her paisley dress, and a matching ribbon gathered her hair loosely at the back of her neck. Watching him walk around the front of the car, Hailey appraised the striking difference between this man dressed in a gray and black tweed sport jacket and black slacks, white shirt, and red tie, and the paint-spattered workman who had opened another door for her. When he slid behind the steering wheel, she smiled. "To quote my great-uncle in Kentucky, 'You clean up right nice, yerself!'"

Cody laughed as he stretched his arm across the back of the seat and turned to back out of the driveway. He lifted his index finger, pointing to her right cheek. "That's turning a really interesting color," he said.

Hailey made a face. "T.J., my nephew, says it matches my shoes."

As they drove onto the country road, Cody said, "He's just jealous. I can remember a few shiners that I was real proud of when I was a kid!"

"Not from doors, I take it."

"One was from a baseball, but the rest were all from fists!"

"You must have been some kid!"

He laughed. "My dad had a full head of brown hair when he married my mother. Six years later he was almost completely gray, and he gives me credit for all of it! You've probably heard a few Christian testimonies that don't leave a dry eye in the house—well, mine is like that."

Hailey turned to face him intently and was surprised by the grin that split his face. "Mine usually evokes tears of *laughter*, however."

Hesitantly, Hailey encouraged, "Go on. . ."

"I was one angry kid after my mother died and I moved here. Looking back, it seems odd that I never felt any anger at Robert—I just took it out on everyone and everything else. I got in with a group of guys who were experts at defacing property. We called ourselves the Graffitis. We blew up mailboxes, broke windows, painted overpasses, that kind of thing. I was sixteen, and one step away from reform school when I got sent to prison for two days. The judge pointed at me and said, 'If this doesn't turn you around, we're going to give up on you, boy!'"

Hailey laughed. "Did it turn you around?"

"Oh, *yeah*! I spent two nights in a cell with a 1200-pound gorilla! This huge bald dude with fingers as big around as my legs was in for armed robbery. He'd become a Christian through a prison ministry, but his persuasive tactics hadn't changed much! As soon as they closed the bars behind me, this big ape picked me up by the armpits, swung me around, and held me up over his head. 'Now listen close, punk,' he said, 'the only way you gonna get outa' this place and stay outa' this place is with Jesus, so you got two days to do some serious changin' or I'm stickin' your head in the toilet!'"

He turned to look into Hailey's wide eyes. "When he finally set me down, I tried telling him that I believed in Jesus and I'd gone to church all my life, but before I knew it I was off my feet again, this time upside-down, staring into the toilet! He said that anyone who really loved Jesus wouldn't hurt Him by ending up in prison. Then he set me down and kept me awake the whole night talking. He didn't have a lot of book knowledge, but he sure knew the Lord. By morning I was on my knees in tears—and it was for real." He paused and grinned at her again. "So, how did you come to be a believer?"

"That's not fair! Who could follow that? Are you sure you didn't make that up?"

"I'm sure. I still keep in touch with him. So, seriously now, tell me about you." Hailey was silent for several minutes. "I came to live with Karlee in January. For a lot of reasons, I wanted to get away from Nebraska for a while. I was running, I guess, from some. . .things. I got into a Bible study at Karlee's church and heard the whole gospel message for the first time—we weren't raised in a church."

Her voice softened and Cody had to lean toward her to catch every word. "It was the message of forgiveness that . . .broke me, I guess. To know that Jesus went through such torture so that I wouldn't have to carry around my guilt—it was so incredible, so freeing." She was quiet again, then added, almost in a whisper, "If only we could forgive ourselves like He does."

⁓

Paige was talking to a customer at the back of the long room as they walked into the gallery, but she managed to exchange a look of anticipation with Hailey.

Cody walked ahead of Hailey to the left side of the room and pointed out a simple pen-and-ink drawing entitled *Pirouette*. He touched the price beneath the frame and shook his head. "To think of all the money I wasted on law school . . .I should have followed in my mother's footsteps!"

Stepping beside him, Hailey nodded. "My niece has done some pretty great stuff in kindergarten—maybe we should start marketing it." They laughed, but Hailey was conscious that hers was a nervous giggle compared to Cody's natural laughter. She was beginning to question their scheme as her eyes connected with Paige, who was walking toward them.

Paige winked at her, but Hailey responded with a worried look. Was she being over-dramatic, putting Cody on the spot? The surprise had kept her smiling to herself all day as she anticipated his reaction. Yet, somehow, standing ten feet from the painting of the Indian woman, her stomach was twisting in knots. Looking up at Paige, Hailey could see that Paige did not share her anxiety.

"I heard that!" Paige whispered in mock indignation. "Please don't let our *serious* customers hear you making fun of our displays," she lowered her voice even more, "or our prices!" She gestured toward a water color. "Now this one should be more to your 'elementary' tastes!"

There were four more pictures that Paige commented on, then stepped back, taking Hailey by the hand as Cody stepped to where the painting of the Indian woman hung in a slight recess in the wall. Hailey gripped Paige's hand and held her breath. Cody froze, then rocked back slightly, almost as from a physical blow.

Hailey pulled her hand away from Paige and went to his side. The look on his face frightened her and she put her hand on his arm. Her voice was barely audible. "Cody?"

She turned to the painting, but Cody's eyes stared back at her from the painted face. The glossy black hair, the long ends blowing in the wind, was held against the woman's temples with a beaded band that echoed the blues in the sky behind her. Her arms were crossed akimbo, and long fringes of white leather fell from them over her slim waist. She was beautiful. The painting was signed simply, "Nita."

A full minute went by before Cody spoke. "Where?" He pulled his eyes away and fixed his gaze on Hailey. "Where did it come from?"

She glanced helplessly at Paige who answered his question.

"New Mexico?" he repeated. He put his hand to his temple, and Hailey felt him waiver. She grasped his arm tighter.

"They were. . .stolen." His voice was hoarse. "All of them. I thought that was. . ." He stopped, taking a deep breath.

The phone rang and Paige bit her lip and nodded to Hailey, then left to answer it.

"Cody," Hailey whispered, "I'm sorry."

He pulled away, his eyes still riveted to the face in front

of him. "I. . .I just need a minute. . ." He turned from her and walked toward the door.

Hailey stared at the painting, at the dark eyes that were Cody's eyes. "Dear God," she whispered, "give me words." On her way to the door, she waved to Paige who was still on the phone. Paige smiled sadly at her and pressed her hands together, telling Hailey that she would pray, then mouthed, "Call me."

He was leaning against her side of the car, facing her as she walked toward him, but not seeing her. Though the evening breeze was warm, his arms were folded in front of him, as if warding off the cold. The click of her heels on the sidewalk roused him and his eyes locked with hers.

"I'm sorry," she repeated when she stood in front of him. "We shouldn't have sprung it on you—I should have told you about it first." Hailey put her hand over his where it rested on his arm. Softly, she added, "I should have realized what feelings this must bring out, what memories. Paige and I were so excited when we were sure it was your mother—I just couldn't wait for you to see it. . ."

He smiled slightly and his eyes sparkled with tears. "Thank you. . . for that." Her hand slid away as he lifted his and gently pulled away the strands of hair that were blowing across her lips. "There's no way you could have known what an impact it would have on me. . .you'd have to know the whole story."

Hailey looked at him expectantly and his smile broadened. His voice was almost a whisper. "I've seen that look before."

A tear slipped from the corner of his eye and she instinctively raised her hand to brush it away. She was touched by his lack of self-consciousness and the trust in his eyes. "Why don't we take a walk," she suggested.

They walked in silence for several minutes, then Cody cleared his throat. "I'm not sure about the time frame— my facts are probably a little jumbled. I've got the memories of a little boy mixed in with what my dad has told me over the years. The robbery must have taken place only a few weeks, maybe days, before my mother died—I know she was in the hospital at the time. Someone broke into the shop in the middle of the night and just about cleaned it out. Dad will know the details. I mostly remember everyone crying—Pampa, Millie, Robert, my mother. . .that was the hardest. I remember feeling how thin she was when I put my arms around her and she was crying. She kept saying, 'They were yours, they were yours. . .'"

Hailey motioned to a bench in a small park just ahead of them. Cody sat beside her and stared down at the key ring in his hand. Twice he took a deep breath and opened his mouth to speak, but stayed silent. Hailey touched his shoulder, trying to give him the courage to continue, and felt him tremble. He turned sideways to face her, then looked down again.

Several minutes went by before he looked up. Tears were on his face and anger in his eyes and voice. "I knew she was dying, but *that*, the robbery, was what killed her."

Hailey nodded, unaware of the tears in her own eyes. "The loss," she whispered, "of her legacy to you. . ."

Cody's right hand clenched in a fist around his keys; his knuckles whitened. "I've tried not to hate, but I'm glad they never caught whoever did it. It's better to blame someone without a face." He was silent for several minutes, then rubbed his hand across his face and sighed. "We'd better go." He smiled softly at her and lifted her chin with the tip of his finger. "Thanks, Little Foot. You're a good listener."

eight

Cody took the paper bag from the girl at the drive-thru window and handed it to Hailey. "This wasn't what I had in mind when I asked you out for dinner," he said.

"This is fine. Besides, I needed that walk far more than I needed a big dinner." She unwrapped a straw and slipped it into his soda. Their eyes met as he took it from her.

"So did I," he said softly.

"What's your next step with the painting? Are you going to try tracing it? Paige and I just assumed that this was one your mother had sold before she died, but. . .wow, this is intriguing. How many were stolen? What if this led to the. . ."

Cody grabbed her left arm and stopped her hamburger in mid-air. She was holding it in both hands, lifting it to her mouth after each sentence, but hadn't yet taken a bite. "Eat, girl! You need your strength to keep up with that mouth of yours!"

Hailey took a bite and tried to look indignant as he winked at her.

"Actually, you voiced the very thoughts that were going through my head. Not that they were moving through my head quite as fast as they were coming out of your mouth. . ."

"Would you like to wear this pickle on your tie tonight?"

"No, thank you." He held out his hand, palm up. "But I will put it over my eye so we match!"

His laughing eyes turned back to the road until something warm and wet dropped onto his hand. "Yecchh!" He reached for his napkin.

"Don't ever tempt me again, Dr. Worth."

"Touché. But don't think for a minute that this is the end of it!"

She grinned wickedly. "Not for a minute."

"Seriously, now," he looked at her arched eyebrow and shook his head. "Seriously, I need to get details from Dad. Would you like to stop over for coffee before I take you home tonight—if it's not too late?"

"I wouldn't miss it, Sherlock."

They finished eating in silence, then Hailey drained the last of her soda and asked, "Do you have any idea what to expect at this meeting?"

"None whatsoever. It's a service organization, a group of philanthropists looking for good causes, I guess. Dad said they were described in an editorial in one of the Madison papers as 'a loose-knit organization of semi-wealthy bleeding heart liberals.'"

Hailey laughed.

"Anyway, I think you and I are the whole program. I was planning on giving some background on the Sparrow Center, then introducing you, and then I'll do a wrap-up when you're done, listing our needs and such, begging for money if they seem receptive. Nervous?"

"Not really. I had an uneventful night at work last night, so I had some time to review. Your dad sent a pile of information with David yesterday, and I have all my school notes and obstetrical and pediatric nursing books here. I made copies of some hand-outs that might be helpful."

"Great. I'm sure you're more prepared than I am. I feel

like a bit of a hypocrite, acting like an expert on something I've only been a part of for a few weeks."

"Just don't tell anyone your real job at the Center is painting walls. It might destroy your credibility!"

Cody laughed. "I had lunch with Dad and David yesterday." He patted the yellow legal pad at his side. "I picked their brains and took lots of notes, and I've got a display in the trunk with pictures of the building, but I'd feel more at ease if this were a Christian group we were addressing. The general public hasn't always been supportive of this project. Dad got some pretty frightening threats when they first started."

"Why? I mean, we're talking about *children*!"

"Not everyone's focus is on the innocent victims. I guess the attitude is 'Why should I be responsible for their mistakes?' Some of the outcry was about bringing 'that kind' of people into the community. The original plan for that land was a huge condominium complex. There were some people who stood to gain a lot of money from it, so I guess you can't blame them.

"Of course, a lot of the animosity comes from people who don't realize that the Center is all privately funded. They assume it's coming out of their pockets. I just don't know what to expect from this group. Let's just pray we appeal to their compassion."

Hailey looked apprehensively at the modern brick building to her right as Cody turned into the parking lot. "But we could be walking into the lion's den."

"Could be!" He smiled and winked again. "We'll just have to ask God to shut their mouths!" He parked the car and turned to face her. "Let's pray before we go in." He took her hand and held it lightly. "Dear Lord, we don't know what to expect tonight. We just put ourselves in Your hands. Please guide our words, and we pray that You'll be glorified by our actions." He squeezed her hand as he said, "Amen."

⋄

"Alcohol is the third leading cause of mental retardation in our country. One baby out of every 750 is afflicted with an identifiable constellation of abnormalities known as FAS, Fetal Alcohol Syndrome. The major features of FAS include craniofacial characteristics such as small head, protruding forehead, slit-like eyes, and a narrow upper lip. Growth retardation and microcephaly are also common. The mean IQ in children born with FAS is about sixty-eight.

"Many more children, about one in every 125 births, suffer from a less severe set of problems which we call Fetal Alcohol Effects. Their life-long challenges may include learning disorders, attention deficit, and poor muscle control."

Hailey paused a moment and swept her eyes across the room of thirty-some people, then fixed her gaze on a pleasant-looking elderly lady with blue-tinted hair in the middle of the audience. "What this means in terms of numbers is that each year in Wisconsin seventy to eighty babies are born with FAS, and between 150 and 200 more are in some way harmed by the effects of alcohol."

She tried to judge the reactions on the faces in front of her as she went on to explain the long-term struggles faced by families and victims of alcohol-related birth defects. Then she went on to the effects of crack and cocaine on unborn babies.

"A cocaine baby loses the ability to orient to a human

voice and face. In fact, the baby may become *more* irritable the more someone speaks to him or tries to mother him. You can imagine the feelings of frustration and inadequacy this creates in a mother, and the negative cycles that result. This is why our goal is to offer support and education for the entire family. By educating a mother, by encouraging her to stick with a drug treatment program while still maintaining as much contact with her child as possible, we can help establish and protect the precious bond between a mother and her child. . ." Hailey's voice grew raspy on the last few words. She took a sip from the glass in front of her and continued. "We can help her break a cycle of poor choices and costly mistakes that may have existed for generations."

There were several nods of agreement as she concluded. The elderly woman smiled at her. Hailey turned to Cody, who took over from there.

Coffee and Danish kringle was made available after the meeting. Cody and Hailey stood near the coffee urn answering questions as people milled about informally. The lady with the blue hair gave Hailey a hug. "God bless you, dear. I was so touched with what you said about helping those women break negative cycles. We can't just support them, we have to show them how to change!"

The tall, balding man next to her scowled. "Oh, Margaret, cut the blarney! These programs don't work—a month later they're back on drugs and back making more babies that somebody has to pay for!" He turned to Cody and scowled again, then apologized to Hailey without sincerity. "I'm sorry, miss, but I just don't see it. Children like that shouldn't be allowed to come into the world in the first place! That's the only way to break those cycles!"

The woman gasped. "Why, Howard!"

The man fixed his cold stare on Hailey. "You're a nurse. There are ways they can tell about. . .abnormalities before birth. Abortion is perfectly safe and legal and should. . ."

"Howard! Murdering a helpless baby is not the answer to the mistakes of his parents!"

"Oh, Margaret, quit being melodramatic!"

Ignoring the man's comment, Cody nodded to the woman. "I agree. Abortion is never a solution." He had more to say, but the veins in the man's neck were bulging, and Cody was in no mood for an argument. He put his arm across Hailey's shoulder to steer her away and was surprised to feel her shaking beneath his arm. He was even more alarmed to feel her stiffen as he drew her closer.

Cody slid beneath the steering wheel and fastened his seat belt. "Well, only one lion in the group wasn't too bad, huh? But people like that sure can get under your skin, can't they?"

"Mm-hm."

"On the whole I think everyone was supportive, don't you?"

"Yes."

"You did a great job. You really know your stuff."

"Thank you. So did you."

"Still up for a cup of coffee?"

"I think I'd better get home. It's late."

Cody stared at her in the dark, opened his mouth, and then changed his mind. "Yeah," he said, "it's been a long day."

nine

"Hailey, over here!" Turning her head, Hailey strained to find Paige, but her voice was lost in the crowd. The reception area of the Sparrow Center was full to capacity. Finally, she caught a glimpse of Paige, making her way toward the punch bowl with a full glass pitcher. Hailey squeezed through, making her apologies as she went.

Reaching Paige she said, "I'll give you a police escort." Walking ahead of her, she called, "Excuse me, make way for the punch."

When they reached the punch table, Paige threw her arms around Hailey, hugging her tight. "Isn't this great?"

The excitement in her voice was contagious. Nodding in agreement, Hailey answered, "It's wonderful! I never imagined a crowd this size. Where did they all come from?"

"Who cares! They're here!" Paige laughed. "Aren't you supposed to be in charge of the guest book?"

"I'm just taking a quick break for some punch. Aren't you supposed to be giving tours?"

Paige waved to someone across the room before answering. "I brought my last group back here and found the bowl empty. Karlee said she'd keep an eye on it, but she's too busy playing hostess with David."

"The mayor just left and a senator just walked in. I've been assigning all the big shots to David and Karlee or Robert for the tour. I think every member of the city council has been here, along with the police chief, the fire chief, and the building inspector. You did a fantastic job with advertising, Paige."

"Thanks. All the big shots got invitations, but most of these people just saw it in the paper. David said he'd be grateful if fifty people showed up."

Hailey shook her head in awe. "There are at least six pages full in the guest book. I'm sure there have been well over a hundred and fifty people already and we've got two hours to go."

"What a miracle," Paige said.

"The decorations are perfect. Everyone's been commenting on them. Did you end up spending the night here? When I left for work yesterday afternoon you were still cleaning!"

Hailey fingered the satin ribbons on the pink linen table cloth beside her and looked around the room. Arched above each doorway was a swag of pink and blue ribbons, tying together two columns of helium balloons twisted together with curled ribbons that swayed softly when anyone passed. Pink and blue balloons hovered on the ceiling, with yards of curled metallic ribbon dancing just above the crowd.

"Do you really think so? I wanted it all to be just right. And, to answer your question, it took a few bags of cheeseburgers and a couple dozen milk shakes to bribe, I mean *reward*, Pastor Anderson's youth group to help last night. They've really been great. Several of them are talking about starting a volunteer program here."

"I talked to a lady from a senior citizen group in town that wants to start a grandparent program. I can't believe how supportive people are being."

"Kinda restores your hope, doesn't it?"

Hailey agreed. "Well, one for the road, and it's back to

work. I'll trade you jobs in a bit if you want."

"Deal. My voice is giving out!"

⋙

Later that evening, Hailey returned to the reception area with a group of ladies from a local church. The crowd had thinned so she was able to point out the mural that covered most of one wall. Tall African grasses in varied shades of green and brown surrounded a giant thorn tree. The women laughed at the playful gray rhino that hid behind the tree, his bulging sides showing on each side. His great horn and one small eye peeked around the tree, and there was a look of triumph on his face. Behind each plant and tree were other animals playing hide-and-seek. A lion with a full, shaggy main stood on his hind feet and leaned against a tree, covering his eyes with huge paws.

"All of the murals in the building were designed by Paige Stern, sister of the architect that designed the Sparrow Center."

There were murmurs of approval from the women. "Such talent!" exclaimed one woman.

"And what a beautiful sense of humor!" said another.

Just then, Hailey caught a glimpse of Paige peering out of the door to Robert's office and pointing in her direction. Her other hand shielded her mouth as she whispered to someone inside the room. The look on her face resembled the mischievous rhinoceros.

Hailey raised her eyebrow and smiled sweetly at the ladies. "Yes, humor is certainly one of her many gifts." As she ushered them to the punch table, she kept one eye on Robert's door.

She didn't have long to wait before Paige approached her, almost breathless with excitement. "Just stay here, there's someone I want you to meet." Before Hailey could even think of a question, she was gone.

Suddenly, in front of her stood a tall, deeply tanned man with thick black hair. Paige was clinging to one arm and he extended the opposite hand to her. "Hello, Hailey."

"Hello," she offered weakly, "I'm Hailey."

Laughing, he replied, "I know."

Only then did Paige begin the introductions. "Hailey, this is Philip, Philip this is Hailey."

Not knowing what was expected of her, Hailey looked from Paige to Philip and back again.

"Finally we've met," he was saying. "I've heard so much about you from my mother and my brother—and of course Paige."

Hailey watched as he patted Paige's hand, wondering what she had missed.

"Stop it, Philip, we're only confusing her. This is my brother, *and* David's brother, and Karlee's soon-to-be brother-in-law, and the man you're going to stand up with at the wedding, Philip Joseph Stern."

"Oh! *Phil*! David and Karlee call you Phil—I didn't recognize the name, and I didn't know you were going to be here. Karlee never mentioned it and. . ."

"You're babbling, Hailey," Paige teased.

"It's what I do best."

Phil laughed. "A family trait, I've heard." He smiled the same inviting smile she had seen so many times on David. "I didn't tell anyone I was coming. I thought it would be fun to surprise everyone."

"A family trait, I've heard!"

Paige interrupted their laughter. "Well, Robert's locking the doors. Why don't you show Philip where the food is before it gets put away—he's starving. He's *always* starving! Then you can join David and Karlee and the kids in the break room."

Hailey handed Phil a small paper plate which he heaped with finger sandwiches and appetizers until it threatened to collapse. Hailey laughed and took the plate out of his hand. Arranging all of his food on an empty serving tray, she added a large slab of layer cake and a handful of mints and nuts and handed it to him.

"Follow me. I'll get you some punch and we'll join the others."

"You're all right, Hailey," he said.

She shrugged. "There are perks to being 'family.'"

As they passed Robert's office, Hailey picked up Cody's voice. Instinctively she turned, only to see Paige sitting next to him in front of Robert's desk, her hand on his arm. Their heads were leaning close together.

Hailey hated the surge of jealously that overtook her, and tried to resist the thought that followed logically: Paige was trying to push her off on Phil so that she could have free access to Cody. The idea shouldn't bother her, she argued; after all, she had purposely distanced herself from him over the past week. She hadn't been cold, just preoccupied, and clearly, he had gotten the message and had pulled back from her too. It had to be, but still it hurt, and seeing him with Paige only made it worse. But there were ways to hide jealousy.

≈

Paige and Cody bent over the two-page fax that had come into Robert's office at the hospital the day before. Across from them, Robert was making notes on a yellow legal pad. Cody nodded that he had finished reading the first page, and Paige put the other paper on top. Suddenly she grabbed his arm.

"Forrest Reed? *The* Forrest Reed? He's the 'other artist' you were talking about? The one whose works were stolen along with your mother's?"

Cody nodded, bewildered, then looked to Robert, who reflected the same look. "You're familiar with his work, I take it?"

"Familiar? Of course! He died about—oh, six months ago, I guess. He was big, I mean really big. His pieces are selling for five digits—and that's just his jewelry and pottery! His paintings. . .Cody, you're sitting on a gold mine, I mean if it hasn't all been sold, even so, you're a lawyer. . .From what you say, those paintings are rightfully yours, and. . ."

She left the papers in Cody's hands and put her hands to her cheeks. "I'm talking like Hailey! I can't think straight! This says that several of Reed's paintings from the sixties have recently appeared on the market, yet they can't be traced to previous owners. . ." She scanned the copy of a newspaper article from a Montana paper. "There's no mention of them having been stolen, though it could be implied. . ." Her eyes lit up. "I bet whoever took them hung onto them until Forrest was gone! After all these years they felt it was safe to sell them, and your mother's paintings. . .if there are more of them. Do you remember any of her other pictures? Can you describe them? I could send fliers out to all of the major galleries."

Robert nodded and rubbed his chin, then tilted his chair back and held the yellow pad up in front of him. "That's a good idea. This fax came from a friend of mine who's a private investigator in California. He's good; I'm confident we'll be hearing more from him soon. And we've already contacted the Missoula Sheriff's Department. One of their officers, a Sergeant Gorman, remembers the case. He was a personal friend of Pampa and Millie, and the first one on the scene after the robbery. He's ready to retire—I think he wants to go out in a blaze of glory, so he's more than willing to put in overtime for us."

Cody took up the story. "A detailed list of everything that was stolen is still on file. We'll check with the sheriff's department about sending it out to the galleries. It seems like a logical first step."

Paige was sitting on the edge of her chair. "This is so exciting--it's like something right out of those mystery novels Hailey is always reading. I bet she flipped when she read this!"

Cody handed the paper back to Robert. With forced casualness he said, "Haven't had a chance to show it to her yet."

The edge in his voice was not lost to Paige. "Well," she said, "she's probably never heard of Forrest Reed anyway."

❧

Hailey was standing in the lobby talking to Phil when Cody and Paige followed Robert out of his office. A bright smile lit Hailey's face when she saw Cody, but the smile was directed at Phil. A little too loudly she said, "I'll be ready at seven, Phil." With a coy wave, she turned back toward the break room, followed closely by Paige.

David had walked into the lobby in time to catch the last line. He raised his eyebrows at Phil. "Two-timing, little brother?"

Phil made a face and shook his head. "Just getting to

know the family. She invited me out for dinner."

When David's eyebrows arched even higher, Phil pulled a small box from his coat pocket. As he opened it, the light caught on the facets of a large marquis diamond. "Laura's birthday present. Any more questions?"

Cody stood in the hallway, close enough to hear every word that had just been said in the lobby and also to eavesdrop on the conversation between Paige and Hailey in the break room.

Paige stood in the doorway, one hand on her hip. "So, what's with you and my brother?"

"Who knows? He's really sweet. We're having dinner tonight!" The sparkle in her eyes looked like it had been pasted there. Paige was confused, but not fooled. She turned and saw Cody staring in her direction. His eyes told her that he'd heard. Paige shrugged, a gesture that told him it didn't make any more sense to her than it did to him.

ten

Karlee stepped into her bedroom, fresh from a shower. A pair of new black sweatpants and a red, white, and black Badger sweatshirt were laid out on the bed. After dressing, she slipped on a pair of red slipper-socks and began brushing her damp copper hair into a pony tail. Her reflection in the oval mirror sent her back to her teens. She felt as giddy as a fifteen-year-old getting ready for a sleepover, though she was sure that tonight's slumber party would be far different than any in her high school years.

Humming to herself, she bent down to open the bedroom window and drank in the cool evening air. The setting sun reflected sparks of light on her diamond. Without thinking, she reached for the phone, sat on the bed, and dialed. As a deep voice answered, she lay back on a pile of pillows, her legs still crossed, and smiled contentedly.

"Hello?"

"Hi, David."

"Did the kids forget something?"

"No. I just missed you."

"I missed you too. How long has it been?"

Looking at the digital clock on her dresser, she sighed, "An hour and forty-nine minutes."

A smooth Cary Grant imitation met her ears. "Tsk, tsk. That long? My, oh my. That would explain your calling."

"Be sensitive, David! You're talking to a woman in love! I can't tell you how many times while you were gone I

67

wanted to call you and hear that voice," she sighed.

"But instead you watched *An Affair to Remember* just one more time. . ."

"Not *that* voice! *Your* voice! And don't you dare make fun of that movie!"

"Who me? Now that *would* be insensitive!"

"Rrrr! So, how are the kids doing without me?"

"They've been good as gold since I promised to take them to Disney World."

"David, you didn't! Unless. . .is that where we're going for our honeymoon?"

"Hah! I'm really getting into this fatherhood business, but there are limits! But I think a 'family' honeymoon would be kind of nice, after we get back. What do you think?"

"I think you're too wonderful," Karlee sighed.

"Just keep thinking like that. Now, hasn't the wedding shower/slumber party of the year started yet? Mom left here about twenty minutes ago."

"I can hear voices downstairs, but they're keeping me a prisoner in this tower until they're ready for me."

David laughed. "So you were calling to see if I would rescue you?"

"Uh-huh."

"Well, I would, but I'm afraid the fries would burn before I got back. Now, if you could call at a more convenient time. . ."

"My hero. . ."

"So what's this call really all about, my dear Kar? Are you sure the kids didn't forget anything?"

"Well, it's your first time taking care of them alone, and it's an overnighter, and. . ."

"And you sound just like my mother! Such trust! Now,

if you don't let me go, I'll never get the corn dogs in the oven!"

"Okay. I love you."

"I love you, too."

"Kiss the kids for me."

"I will."

"What are they doing now?"

David laughed. "They're putting together the electric train that my dad bought them."

"He's going to be a good grampa."

"Yes, he is," David agreed patiently. "Now, good night, dear."

"Your mom's going to be a good gramma, too."

"Yes, she is. Good night."

"Did your dad go to the game with Robert?"

"Yes, he did. Good night."

"So you really are alone. I could drive over now, you know."

"I know you could."

"I will. . ."

"No, you won't." His voice grew quiet. "Kar?"

"Hm?"

"Thank you for letting me be a father."

"This is just the beginning."

"I can't wait to get started on the rest."

"And how many do you have in mind, Mr. Stern?"

"Two. What would you say to two more?"

"I'd say, do you mind becoming a new daddy before our first wedding anniversary?"

"I couldn't think of a better gift."

"Speaking of honeymoons. . ."

"We weren't."

"David, I don't even know how to pack!"

"Hailey and Paige do."

"This isn't fair!"

"Humor me. Our honeymoon is my gift to you."

"I'm not going to know anything?"

"I hope nothing! Just trust me on this, Kar."

"I trust you in everything, David."

"Even with your kids?"

"Even with our kids."

"Then say good night and let me bake my corn dogs."

"I could come over and help. . ."

"Say good night."

"Good night."

"I love you, Karlee."

"I love you, too." Holding the receiver close to her cheek she listened for the soft click on the other end of the line.

⟩⟩

Karlee covered her eyes with one hand as she came down the stairs. Hailey's voice rose up to greet her. To the tune of the Miss America theme song, she sang, "Here she is'. . .Mrs. David Stern (almost). . . Here she is, my. . . sister. . ."

Karlee waved her arm. "Stop!" she laughed, "you sing worse than you cook!"

Hailey reached for Karlee's arm and steered her in the direction of the women waiting comfortably in the living room. Bowing slightly, Hailey said, "Since some of your guests just arrived, will you do us the honor of making introductions?"

Karlee put her arm around Hailey who was dressed in maroon hospital scrubs. "Of course, this is my crazy sister, Hailey Austin. And over in the rocking chair in the pink satin pajamas, is my future mother-in-law, Rose Stern. Hiding behind the steps is my soon-to-be sister-in-law and Hailey's new roommate, the artist, Paige Stern." Paige had on a long white night shirt and knee-high-boot slippers.

"And on the sofa my two dear friends—Jody Hansen, in the red sweats, and Edna Kosinski, my Bible study leader and David's second mother, who is knitting an afghan for one of her favorite men even as we speak."

Edna was wearing a long flannel nightgown and a pair of her husband's wool socks. Already her knitting needles were clicking in the air with strands of white yarn between them as she hurried to finish the blanket she had promised David as a wedding present. She smiled up at Karlee. "It's for you too, dear."

Karlee returned her smile, then turned to Hailey. "It's all yours, sis."

"Thank you, my dear sister. Paige and I want to thank everyone for coming and sharing this evening with Karlee before she is carried off by her knight in shining armor. Now, everyone in the dining room. We're going to start with spinach quiche and crescent rolls, accompanied by a fresh fruit salad and followed by a selection of flavored coffees and herb teas to go with the chocolate-raspberry cheese cake."

Murmurs of approval met Hailey's announcement, and grew as the women took their places at the table. Candlelight shimmered off Karlee's white china and crystal goblets filled with sparkling red cranberry juice.

"I'm impressed!" Karlee said. "Somehow, I was expecting pizza or sub sandwiches. Aren't we a bit underdressed?"

"Not at all," Paige answered. "After Hailey and I put so much time and effort into preparing this meal, we wanted you all to be comfortable while you enjoyed it."

"Why don't I believe a word of this?" Karlee laughed.

"Because," Rose said, "rumor has it that your sister can't cook any better than my daughter." She accented her comments with a doleful look at Paige.

Hailey put her arm on Paige's shoulder. "Can you believe this? After you got up at four this morning to start on the rolls, and I went out and picked the spinach by hand, and this is the thanks we get?"

Edna gestured toward the kitchen. "Wasn't that a box from Van's Deli I saw on the counter?"

As Paige and Hailey tried to look crestfallen, the others laughed.

Rose wiped at her eyes, damp from laughing so hard. "Well, thanks to our dear Karlee here, I'm finally going to be a gramma. There's not much hope of my daughter snaring a husband with her culinary charms!"

The phone rang just as Edna finished asking the blessing. Karlee waved Jody over to the phone, "Its Don. The boys want to say good night."

Knowing smiles followed Jody as she shook her head and walked to the kitchen.

"It's nice to be needed, isn't it?" Edna said sweetly.

Coffee cups were filled and carried into the darkened living room after dinner. Only the soft glimmer of light from the fireplace lit the room.

"I've asked Edna to give a devotional later tonight, some of her 'words of wisdom' from forty-seven years of marriage. We could let Karlee open her gifts now, but I think we'll make her wait till around midnight," Hailey said, smirking at Karlee. "Right now, we have a decision to make." She pointed to Paige who held up two video cassettes. "Will it be *Casablanca* or *An Affair to Remember*?"

"Definitely *An Affair to Remember*," Rose answered. Edna and Jody quickly agreed.

"All right, *An Affair to Remember* it is," Paige said, setting the other tape down, then adding in her best Bogart voice, "We'll play it another time, Sam."

By the time the credits rolled on the screen the Kleenex box had been passed around several times. Dabbing her eyes, Rose sighed, "I've always loved that movie. I can remember the first time Raymond and I saw it."

Taking the Kleenex box from her mother, Paige said, "It's the first time I've ever seen it."

Edna looked reflective for a moment, then made a perfect segue into her devotional. "You know, life isn't like the movies. Love is not a feeling, but an act of our will. Take a look at I Corinthians 13," she said, as she quoted from memory. 'Love suffers long. That means patience, being slow to anger, putting up with dirty socks on the floor and whiskers in the sink, as well as the big things. Love is kind. Love does not seek its own, it is not selfish. That means going a hundred per cent to meet your mate's needs, none of this fifty-fifty stuff! Love bears all things, it has no end to its trust. Love believes all things, hopes all things, endures all things. Love never fails.' So many people today don't know how to identify genuine love because they don't know how to define it in the first place!"

"Amen!" Rose agreed.

Jody sipped her caramel nut coffee. "I've only heard parts of that before—it makes so much sense. Don is one of the most unselfish men I know. I love him for that. Where is that in the Bible, again?"

Rose lifted the Bible off the end table, found I Corinthians, and laid the open book on Jody's lap. "Edna, that was said beautifully. I can see why my son thinks so much of you. Now I'd like to read Proverbs 31, if that's all right."

The others nodded as she pulled a mauve-colored Bible case from the tote bag at her feet and put on her reading glasses. She opened her Bible, then removed her glasses and looked up. "Karlee, I hope this isn't inappropriate, but I just need to express my gratitude. Raymond and I began praying for our children and their future families even before they were born. To think of how God has blessed us with two beautiful women who have loved the Lord and treasured our son. . ." She wiped a tear from her cheek. "I'm afraid my faith wavered at times over the last four years—I wondered if David would ever know happiness again. And now, tonight, to see the joy on his face as he sat on the floor playing with your two precious children. . ." Rose took a moment to steady her voice, and Karlee slipped over to wrap her arms around her. "Thank you, Karlee."

The mood was broken by the ringing phone. Karlee whispered, "Thank you," and went to answer it.

Jody laughed while dabbing at her eyes. "Now whose man is that? Yours, Edna? Or maybe David—it wouldn't surprise me."

Paige returned from the kitchen with a fresh pot of coffee and a pan of homemade fudge Edna had made. Behind her walked Karlee. "Phone's for you, Hailey. It's Cody."

eleven

Shifting the cordless phone to his right ear, Cody paced his small kitchen, opened the back door, and walked out onto the back porch. He wiped his damp palm on his faded jeans, sat on the step, then stood abruptly as Hailey came on the line.

"Uh, hi!" he stammered, feeling anything but the confident lawyer. "I just thought I ought to give you an update . . .unless Paige has already filled you in. . .about the paintings?" The statement came out like a question, so he paused for Hailey to answer.

"No. She said you'd uncovered some more information. She thought I should ask you about it."

Cody nodded to himself. *And why didn't you?* he wondered.

"Have you got a minute?" he asked.

There was a slight pause. "Sure," she said politely.

He thought of the times they had passed in the hall at the Sparrow Center over the last week. He had a question he had to ask even though it didn't fit into the conversation he had started. "By the way, have you heard from Phil since he got back?"

"No."

It was the answer he was hoping for, but it didn't solve much. The scene in the lobby five days earlier had been very poor acting on her part, but why had she done it? What was she trying to prove? Looking out across the field at the smudge of pink that was settling on the horizon, Cody said a quick prayer. *Lord, what have I done wrong? Please help me with this*.

"Is this a bad time?"

"Well, we've got company, but I've got a few minutes. I really do want to hear what you've come up with."

Her voice had thawed some, and he heard a hint of genuine interest. Cody breathed a sigh of relief.

"Dad has a friend who's a P.I. in northern California. He flew to Montana last week and he's sent us some intriguing information. At the time of the robbery there were three other artists besides my mother who had their work for sale at the shop. One of them was Forrest Reed. Ever heard of him?"

"No, but that doesn't mean anything."

"Well, Dad and I hadn't either, but Paige says he's become quite famous in the last twenty years. Anyway, he died a few months ago, and since then at least six of his early paintings have shown up on the market. They were all dated and some go back to the early sixties. Well, Dad just talked to this friend of his a few minutes ago, and the descriptions of the paintings that have recently sold match the ones on the list filed with the sheriff's office after the robbery."

"Wow! Any clues on where they're coming from?"

"Not really. They were all sold west of the Rockies, but all the way from Montana to Texas, each in a different state, each with a different name for the seller. It's hard to tell how many people we're dealing with here."

"Sounds to me like a pretty organized network."

Cody smiled, warmed by the enthusiasm in her voice. "Paige says you're into mysteries."

"Don't laugh! I've learned a lot from reading—who knows, maybe I'll solve this thing for you!"

"Nothing would surprise me with you!" Cody said, then cringed with fear that the comment had been too personal. He had a fleeting memory of a frightened kitten he had tried to coax out of Pampa's shed when he'd been a child. He had the distinct impression that Hailey needed to be approached with the same gentleness, though he didn't know why.

There was silence on Hailey's end, and Cody nervously tried to fill it. "There should be seven more of Reed's paintings, according to the sheriff's report. They're selling for upwards of twenty grand a piece."

"So if they can be found before they're sold, someone is in for a nice surprise! Did this Reed guy have a family?"

"Yes, but. . .well, it's kind of complicated."

"I'm listening."

Cody laughed. He quit pacing, sat back down on the top step, and leaned against the door. Closing his eyes, he mouthed, *Thank you, Lord.* He took a deep breath and said out loud, "Well, Dad remembers meeting Reed at the shop a couple years before he married my mother. He was a local kid, trying to put himself through college. Pampa recognized his potential and was kind of a mentor, just like he was to my mother. Anyway, to help him pay for tuition, Pampa agreed to buy all of his work outright, instead of selling on consignment like he usually did."

"So the paintings actually belonged to Pampa."

"Right. And because Pampa and Millie didn't think Lyle, the nephew I told you about, could be counted on to manage the shop if something happened to them, they had it put in their will that it would go to my mother."

"Did they change it after your mother died?"

Cody paused. "Yeah. They had the shop put in my name, with Dad to act as overseer until I came of age."

"Whoa. . .Cody, think about it! Remember what you said about wishing you didn't have student loans to pay off, about wanting to go into the mission field full time?"

"You're jumping ahead a bit!"

"I know, but just think about the possibility! What if they find the paintings and you sell them for a couple hundred thousand, and. . ."

"Slow down, girl! I'm trying not to let greed enter into this!"

"I'm sorry." Hailey's laugh broadened Cody's smile. "Well, I guess the best thing is that you may be getting close to finding the rest of your mother's paintings."

"That's a better focus. But it's not like I haven't had some interesting speculations about what the Lord is going to do with this." Cody tilted his head back and closed his eyes. "I suppose I should let you get back to your company." He took a deep breath. "Hailey?"

"Hm?"

"Thanks for listening again," he said softly. "I've missed you."

There was a long pause. Her voice was strained and low as she said, "I'll see you later."

Cody stared at the phone, then set it down on the step next to him. The sky had turned a deep slate blue with only a thin line of violet still visible between the trees. He was surrounded by the familiar sounds of a summer evening, but the chirping of the crickets and the bull frogs croaking in the pond were not soothing sounds tonight. Cody was intent on analyzing his reactions to Hailey's mood changes, trying to comprehend her affect on him. The result was only deeper confusion.

Something about her pulled at him. He labeled it a kindred spirit, though that made little sense. The physical attraction was easy to understand, but he felt more for her than that. He smiled to himself as he remembered standing outside the gallery, brushing her hair off her face. She was beautiful, in a casual way that appealed to him. The whimsical hat she had worn the day of her interview was the first thing that had attracted him. It had spoken of a childlike sense of humor that he had had glimpses of up until their trip to Madison.

The second thing that had caught his attention was the fire in her eyes when he had laughed about the paint on her face that first day. He knew he'd met a competent match in the woman with the purple cheek, glaring up at him with her hands on her hips.

But he had been attracted before, many times before. What made this time different? Once again, his thoughts drifted to their walk in the park, and for the first time a piece of the puzzle seemed to fit.

He had been vulnerable with Hailey; after knowing her for less than a week, he had willingly shared things with her that he had never told anyone. He felt her hand on his arm, saw the tears in her eyes, and it suddenly all made sense.

She had a quality of selflessness that he had rarely seen, even in the Christian women he had dated. She had hurt for him, with him, and it had melted his reserve. And now he needed, somehow, to do the same for her.

He lowered his head, his fists clenched as he pleaded for wisdom. The last few minutes of their time at the community center replayed before him, and the Lord opened his eyes. As he picked up the phone again, he prayed, *Father, help me walk it with her*.

&

Questioning eyes met Hailey when she walked back into the living room. Rose and Edna, who would be sleeping in the upstairs bedrooms, were settled on the couch with afghans, and Karlee, Jody, and Paige were crawling into sleeping bags on the floor. Jody was the first to speak.

"So who's Cody?"

Reading some hesitation on her sister's face, Karlee stepped in. "He's Robert Worth's son. Adopted son, actually. He just finished his doctorate in law, and he's working for the Center for a few months."

"How old is he?"

Karlee shook her head and looked at Hailey.

"Twenty-nine," she answered.

"Single?" Jody persisted.

Paige was also sensing Hailey's mood, and answered for her. "Yes, he's tall, dark, handsome, and single, Jody, but you're already married."

Before Jody could reply, Paige stood and announced that it was finally time for Karlee to open her gifts. Piling boxes on Karlee's lap, Paige said, "We figured that, between the two of you, you have more household stuff than you need, so we thought a personal shower was in order."

Hailey, beginning to relax again, added, "And David agreed."

Rolling her eyes, Karlee laughed, "I'll just bet he did!"

She opened the box from her future mother-in-law first, and gasped at the pink chiffon peignoir. "Oh, Rose, I. . . it's so beautiful!"

Edna's gift was next and was a perfect reflection of the giver. Karlee reached up to give her a hug as she held the long pink flannel gown against her chest. Edna said, "Well, dear, you have to be a little practical some of the time!"

Opening the third box, Karlee's cheeks flushed as she held up the red silk teddy. "This has to be from Paris!"

Paige nodded. "I picked it out before I left." She gave a mischievous grin, looking first at Karlee and then at her mother. "I just want my big brother to be happy!"

With a measure of trepidation, Karlee ripped the wrapping paper off the gift from Hailey. "This scares me, little sister," she said, pulling the top off the box, then dissolving into laughter at its contents. She stood up, holding it in front of her. "Now, *this* I have to try on!"

Karlee ran into the bathroom, then returned to model her new one-piece, footed sleeper, complete with a buttoned "trap door" over her bottom. Karlee gave Hailey a hug amid all the laughter, then sat down cross-legged on her sleeping bag and sighed. "This has been so much fun— thank you, all of you."

Paige looked at Hailey, and Hailey nodded. "You're not done yet." Paige reached behind the couch and pulled out another box. Karlee looked at her questioningly as she opened the small envelope taped to the top. Inside the card, in very familiar handwriting, were the words, "I'll never try to change you. I love you just the way you are. David."

A collective "Aw. . ." went up from the group as Karlee read the words out loud. She lifted the cover and grinned as tears stung her eyes. Beneath the tissue paper was an emerald green sweat suit, trimmed with white lace and pale green pearls. Tucked in the lace at the neck was a small card which read, "I love you in green."

twelve

"What's wrong with this picture?" Paige asked as she walked into David's bedroom carrying her camera.

"Absolutely nothing," Karlee answered innocently.

"I don't know. . .a beautiful woman in her wedding dress with a pile of sheets and blankets in her arms. . .looks odd."

Karlee laughed. "The Bible says we're a peculiar people."

"Some a little more than others," Paige muttered, framing Karlee in a square made by her fingers.

Stripping the bed, Karlee tossed the sheets on the floor, then bent to stretch the corners of the fitted sheet over the mattress.

Paige stepped around the open door to stand in front of the full-length mirror. She adjusted the shoulders of the filmy coffee-colored dress and brushed her hair from her eyes, all the while watching Karlee walk around the four-poster bed, fitting corners and smoothing out the creases on the crisp white sheets.

Karlee clamped a pillow beneath her chin as she slipped on a pillow case. Through jaws almost closed she explained, "I didn't think David would remember to do this and I want everything to be perfect when we get back from wherever we're going."

"You're probably right. David wouldn't think of it," she smiled slowly, "but Mom did. . .about nine o'clock this morning. She changed the sheets, put clean towels in the bathroom. . ."

Karlee dropped the second pillow. "Paige, you could have stopped me!"

"You were way past 'stop' when I came in," Paige laughed.

"You and Hailey are going to make great roommates—you're both so experienced in the fine art of torture!"

Paige answered with a villainous laugh. "My bags are packed and I'm ready to start making her life miserable before you get back!"

Karlee shook her head as she picked up a large plastic bag, pulled out a navy and burgundy lone-star quilt and set it gently on the bed. Paige ran her hand across the no-wale corduroy with satin insets, then bent for a closer look at the tiny hand stitches. "You do beautiful work, Karlee," she said seriously, then nodded toward a small quilt hanging on the wall next to the French doors. It looked like a four-paned window, depicting the four seasons, and had been a gift to David from Karlee the night of their first date. "I don't think David ever looks at that without getting misty-eyed."

Her eyes dampened as she spoke the words and Karlee put her arms around her. "You take good care of my big brother," Paige sniffed.

"I will."

"I've missed. . .I've always wanted a sister."

Karlee leaned toward the Kleenex box on the nightstand, pulling Paige with her and making her giggle through her tears. Handing her a tissue, Karlee said, "Well, now you've got two of them. . .and so do I. Now quit sniffling on my wedding dress!" She dabbed at her own eyes as Paige helped her unfold the quilt.

"Are my parents and Hailey here yet?" Karlee asked.

"Hailey called a while ago. They should be here any minute. Your mom's bringing your 'something old.' Do you know what it is?"

"Yes," Karlee nodded, "it's a pearl teardrop necklace that my grandmother wore on her wedding day. My mother wore it and Hailey will too."

Paige sighed. "I love traditions."

Karlee smiled and wrinkled her nose. "You, my almost-sister, are the most *un*traditional person I know!"

With a shrug, Paige defended herself. "Well, weddings make me nostalgic. Who knows, I might surprise everyone and have a very traditional wedding myself someday."

"Not a chance! I picture you saying 'I do' beneath the Arc de Triomphe in bare feet, with a rose between your teeth!"

Paige grabbed a pen off David's dresser and held it between her teeth, twirling around in front of the mirror. Over their laughter they heard the chimes of the door bell. Paige stopped, leaned toward Karlee, and whispered, "Well, just between us, if Hailey is telling the truth about losing interest in a certain 'tall, dark, and handsome,' Paris may lose its appeal come fall."

Karlee raised her eyebrows. "My sister's a little gun-shy, I think, but I don't think your competition's throwing in the towel yet."

"Don't worry, as long as there's even a spark of interest I'm keeping my distance. Her friendship is too important." Paige paused, then added, "I can torture her in other ways!"

Karlee shook her head, then changed the subject. "Are David's suitcases downstairs?"

"Already in the trunk of the car. Wait—stop. . .stand there. No, a little to the right. Good." She grabbed her camera, adjusted the lens, and snapped a picture, then settled in the wing-back chair with the camera on her lap.

Karlee closed the closet door after storing David's old comforter on a shelf and moved across the room to the low chest of drawers next to the high-boy dresser. Reaching inside a small print bag, she began to arrange lotion bottles, make-up jars, and perfume on the dresser top. As she pulled out a handful of combs and brushes, Paige said, "Do you have a coat tree and mirror in there, Mary Poppins?"

"Very funny, I'll have you—" The door burst open and Shelly flew in, pulling her grandmother behind her.

Ruth Austin was momentarily speechless at the sight of her older daughter. A picture flashed in her mind of a younger Karlee in a long white wedding gown years before, but as she stared at the woman in the ivory lace dress in front of her, the smile on her daughter's face pushed aside any glimmer of sadness. The smile was what finally brought words to her lips. "You look beautiful, honey," she whispered, "absolutely beautiful." She took a moment to steady her voice. "Now turn around so I can put this on you."

Karlee bent her knees to her mother's height as the pearl necklace slipped around her neck. "Is Dad coming up?"

"No, he's waiting for you at the bottom of the stairs. He's strutting like a peacock down there—I don't know if it's because his little girl's getting married or because he was able to get into his uniform again!" She turned to include Paige in the conversation. "It's been eight months since his stroke, and he's complained about his new diet and exercise every single day, but now he's seeing the benefits." She turned Karlee around and looked approvingly at her. "Like you keep telling us, 'All things work together for good.'" Ruth wiped at the tears that slid down her cheeks.

"Oh, Mom, don't get us all started."

Hailey walked in, wearing a peach dress, identical to Paige's except for the color. She was followed by Rose, who motioned for Karlee to turn around. Shelly squealed as her mother did a slow pirouette. "Oh, Mommy, you for sure look like a queen now!" Shelly hugged her gently around her waist, being careful not to crush the dress.

"Okay, do we have something old, something new, something borrowed, and something blue?" Paige asked.

Touching the necklace her mother had put on her, Karlee said, "I have Gramma's necklace, I borrowed Hailey's shoes, and the dress is new."

Rose took a small package out of her purse and handed it to Karlee. "Just a little something to welcome you into our family."

With shaking fingers, Karlee parted the folds of tissue paper and lifted a gold bracelet studded with blue sapphires. She put her arms around Rose. "Thank you Rose. It's breathtaking."

Hailey descended the stairs behind Karlee. Holding her bouquet of daisies, tiger-lilies, and babies' breath in one hand, she reached out to squeeze her father's shoulder and exchanged winks with him as Karlee took his arm and turned into the living room. Philip held out his arm to her and she walked beside him to the fireplace where he led her to Karlee's side and then stepped back to stand next to David.

As Hailey turned to stand at the angle they had practiced, she saw Cody in the first row of folding chairs. He wore a cream-colored linen suit with a dark brown silk shirt. A triangular piece of tiger's eye on a silver disk held together the leather strings of his bolo tie. His hair hung free and shone in the soft light from the candelabras on each side of the room. But it was his eyes, black and deep, that held Hailey. She tried to look away, but something in his eyes commanded her, enveloped her. He stared back, then smiled softly, almost sadly.

Finally, she forced herself to turn from the message she could read so clearly in his eyes. He was pleading silently for her to let him in, something she knew she could never do. That realization hit her with a fresh wave of remorse and longing, making her barely able to concentrate on the ceremony.

She stared at Karlee's profile, at the high color in her sister's cheeks and the softness in her expression. *Lord, make them happy.* She bent and untied David's ring from the white satin pillow T.J. held out to her. T.J. sat down next to her parents and Shelly, who looked like a princess in her white dress trimmed in pale peach ribbons, a basket of flower petals on her lap. *Keep them safe; help them to bind together as a family. Lord, they've known so much sorrow. . .*She swiped at a tear. *Thank You for bringing them together—they deserve this happiness.*

As she took Karlee's bouquet from her, she looked again at Cody, and once again felt a sense of shame. How could she have ever entertained the thought that the same happiness might someday be hers? Hailey clapped with the other guests when Pastor Grander pronounced David and Karlee man and wife, and David took his new wife in a long embrace.

The pastor announced, "I now present to you Mr. and Mrs. David Stern," and Hailey pretended that the tears she pressed against her sister's cheek were tears of joy.

≈

Edna and Jody set out ham sandwiches, potato salad, and relishes, while Jody's husband Don alternated between the video camera and still pictures of the bride and groom and their families. After watching David and Karlee cut the cake, Hailey went out to the kitchen to get an aspirin from her purse. The back of her neck was tight and her head was beginning to throb. As she turned back toward the living room, she jumped as she ran into Cody.

He put a steadying hand on her shoulder. "Sorry, didn't mean to scare you." He bent to look in her eyes. "Are you okay, Little Foot? You look kinda pale."

The tears that hadn't been far from the surface all afternoon threatened again. She looked away from him. "Just a headache. All the excitement, I guess. I just took some aspirin."

His hand, which had never left her shoulder, slid up to the base of her neck. "I do a pretty good neck massage," he offered.

Hailey looked up at his sympathetic smile, then closed her eyes. What would be so wrong with letting down her guard for just a minute? She let her shoulders relax beneath the warmth of his hand and nodded.

Cody motioned for her to sit down on a kitchen chair, but at that moment, Karlee burst into the room. "Hailey, I need you to do me a big favor! I forgot my gift for David . . .the pocket watch. It's in my top right drawer. Could you run and get it for me? Please?"

Hailey took a deep breath. Karlee's entrance had been like a splash of cold water. "Of course. I'll be back in twenty minutes."

Karlee gave her a quick squeeze. "Thanks. I owe you one."

"I'll give you a ride," Cody said.

Forcing a smile, Hailey shook her head. "No, you get back to the party. Thanks, anyway." Grabbing her purse, she headed for the door before she had a chance to weaken again.

thirteen

Digging both hands deep into the pockets of his worn jeans, he fingered the few coins that rested on the bottom. As he looked out from the enclosed porch at the barn and the driveway, occupied now by a black and chrome Harley-Davidson, he wondered how long he should wait. Restless, he paced the length of the front porch before choosing a wicker chair in the corner, half hidden in the shadows. Leaning his head back, he closed his eyes, replaying in his head the last several months.

He could not remember a time he had felt this tired, physically and mentally exhausted. He breathed in the fresh spring air; bending over, he rested his elbows on his knees, running both hands through sand-colored hair long overdue for a haircut. The hair fell over his eyes as soon as he pulled his hand away, a soft golden wave against his tanned skin.

The Jeep pulled almost silently into the driveway. He watched, half wanting to leave. He felt like a cornered animal, trapped between her and his own doubts. He willed her to use the front door. If she did, he would leave. He'd come back tomorrow when her sister was home. Maybe.

He stood and watched her, saw her clench her fist as she walked toward the bike, then stop, and turn back to her car. He breathed a sigh and sunk back into the shadows.

Suddenly, the back door flew open. He stood to face her as words assaulted him like sand thrown in the wind.

"What are you doing here? You can't just barge in here and mess up our lives any time you feel like it! This is Karlee's wedding day, and you're not going to spoil it! Why are you here? Answer me!" On the verge of hysteria, Hailey shook her head, then covered her face with her hands as tears streamed down behind them.

Knowing full well the possible consequences, Randy stepped slowly toward her and gently put his arms around her. Surprising them both, Hailey rested her head on his chest until she had relinquished the anger and pain she had carried for so long.

Softly into her hair, he whispered, "I'm sorry, Hailey, so very sorry. I came here to tell you that. Can we sit down? Will you hear me out, please?"

Hailey stood back, crossing her arms across her chest, and watched him sit, his outstretched hand offering the chair next to him. She sat down across from him, and Randy began repeating out loud the words that had played in his head for weeks.

Shadows danced around them as the afternoon sun slipped below gray clouds. Throughout the beginning of his explanation Hailey remained silent. Then, lifting her hand to stop him, she heard her own voice say, "Let's go inside; there's coffee made."

At the kitchen table, he watched her fill two cups from the coffee pot and reheat them in the microwave. He elected to leave his worn leather jacket on. When she sat down, Randy asked if he could continue. She nodded her head.

"Well, like I was saying, I got a job with a roofing company in Dallas in January. We got a contract to put a new roof on a building downtown. I didn't pay much attention, it was called a women's health clinic, or something like that. It didn't mean anything to me. The third day we were there there was a crowd gathering across the street, and I realized the place was an abortion clinic.

"My first reaction was that, finally, something exciting might happen. I'd seen things on T.V., and I expected to hear yelling and screaming, and people being carried off by the police. But it was nothing like that. All at once, this whole crowd of people knelt down and they started praying and singing. We laughed at them at first. When we took a break, we sat on the edge of the roof like we were watching a football game. We saw women come in and out, but the way the laws are, the protesters couldn't get close to them, so nothing happened.

"I was the last one to leave that afternoon." He paused and looked down self-consciously. "This is where it gets weird. I was walking to my bike and there was this girl heading for the entrance. I almost walked past her, but I noticed she was crying. I don't usually get involved with strangers, but for some reason I asked her if she was okay. She said 'no' and then she started sobbing." Randy took a deep breath to steady his voice. "That's when it hit me. I've always been pro-choice, I suppose, but I never gave it much thought. But that girl could have been you! I never thought about what you went through, how hard it must have been, and all because I never thought about anything but myself!" His eyes shimmered with tears as he finished.

"What happened to the girl?" Hailey asked quietly, wiping a tear from her chin.

"Before I knew what I was doing, I had my arm around her, and I said I thought the people across the street could help her. She didn't argue, so I walked her over to them. There was a lady there who worked at a maternity home, and the girl ended up going home with her."

He paused and stared down at his hands. "I. . .I was

crying by the time I got back to my bike. That's not something I do. . .ever. I knew I had to come back and tell you how sorry I am, for all of it. Nothing should have happened that night, and then to leave you to make that decision alone. . .I'm so sorry."

Hailey wiped her cheeks with her hands, then took a sip of her coffee, all the while keeping her eyes on the place mat in front of her. "You didn't know."

They were silent for several minutes. Hailey curled and uncurled the edge of the place mat while Randy fingered the zipper on his jacket. Finally, he spoke again. "Karlee tried to talk to me about God when I was here in November. I've never been into religion, but she said she'd pray for me, and I have this weird feeling like, I don't know . .like God is cornering me, making things happen, you know? Like working on that clinic—it's too much of a coincidence. Does that make any sense?"

Hailey nodded, then rose silently, walked to the counter, and picked up her Bible, then reached for the phone. After she dialed, she turned and faced Randy squarely for a moment, watching him cup the coffee mug between his hands as if to warm himself.

"Hi, this is Hailey. Could I speak to Karlee please? No, I'm fine. Yes, I'm sure." Turning from Randy, she shut her eyes tight. *Why did Cody have to answer the phone?* "Kar, I just wanted to let you know I'll be a little late. . .No, I'm okay, just a little headache. I think if I just relax for a few minutes I'll be fine. I'll be back long before you leave."

&

Hailey had washed her face and put on fresh make-up after Randy had left, but she knew she looked terrible. If anyone questioned her, she wouldn't have to lie about a headache. She handed the gift to Karlee and went through the motions of having a good time for the next hour. After seeing David and Karlee off, she helped Jody and Paige carry trays of food out to the kitchen while Cody and Robert folded up the chairs to be returned to the church.

Her father walked in, looking years younger in his uniform, and she gave him a hug. "We've been talking with David's parents and Dr. Worth," he said, "and we decided not to waste these good clothes. We're going to drive up to Madison and get a tour of the art gallery, and then go out for a late dinner. How does that sound?"

Her mother walked in just as she started to answer. "Oh, Dad, I really don't feel like it. I've had a headache all afternoon, and I think I'd just like a little down time." She smiled at her mother's worried expression. "I'm really all right, Mom, just exhausted. It's not easy getting a sister married, you know! You two go on and have a great time. I've got jeans in the car, and I'll just putt around here, putting stuff away."

As she was saying good-bye to them at the door, she heard Cody talking to his father outside. "You go on, I'll take David's truck and get this stuff back to the church, and then come back for my car," he said. "I'm not really in the mood for any more partying today, anyway."

Hailey changed into jeans and a lavender T-shirt. She had forgotten to bring different shoes, so she padded around David's kitchen in her bare feet. Her mind was numb, and she felt drained. She was grateful for the silence.

Her headache was finally beginning to ease when she made one final trip into the walk-in pantry with a bag of leftover sandwich buns. As she set them on a shelf, she heard something behind her and turned.

Cody was standing in the doorway of the pantry, one hand on each side of the doorjamb. She took a controlled breath, conscious of the rise in her pulse. She managed a smile.

"Hi! Get the chairs back to the church okay?"

He nodded, said nothing, and continued to stare.

"There's plenty of cake left. Want some?"

He shook his head. She stared up at him; there was nowhere else to look. His collar was open, the sleeves of his shirt rolled to his elbows. His voice was low and husky when he finally spoke. "Talk to me, Hailey."

She fought the tears. "I. . .can't." She tried to push past him but he didn't move, so she backed away from him, against the cupboard.

"Talk to me." The softness in his voice broke her. It was everything she ached for, and everything she couldn't have.

"I can't!" She screamed it. "I can't!" The sobs tore from her, and she slid to the floor. Then, somehow, she was cradled in Cody's arms, curled on his lap like a child, as he rocked her slowly, whispering in her hair.

"It's okay, Hailey. I know, and it's okay."

"You *don't* know, and you *can't* know," she sobbed into his shoulder.

He let her cry, then gently pulled the damp wisps away from her face. His hand nestled in her long hair, and just his thumb rested on her cheek. "You had an abortion, didn't you?" he said.

She stared up at him, searching his eyes, her tears still flowing. "How did you know?" she whispered.

"It all came together after I talked to you last Friday. I was praying for you, and suddenly I knew. I knew why you didn't want to work in the nursery, and why that talk at the community center bothered you, and why you've been avoiding me—maybe even why you pretended to be interested in Phil."

Hailey almost smiled. "That was pretty stupid. We never did end up going out."

Cody brushed his lips across the top of her head. "I'm glad," he whispered.

Her head rested back on his shoulder. She was too spent to move. His hand stroked her hair, and his cheek rested on top of her head. "You know God has forgiven you, don't you?" She nodded. "But you haven't forgiven yourself."

"I can't. . .

"You have to let yourself grieve, Hailey. You have to talk about it. Does anyone know? Karlee, or Edna?"

"No. Just the. . ." she struggled for the right word, "the father."

"Were you in love with him?"

"No. It was a one night stand—we'd been drinking . . . He never even knew I was pregnant, and he didn't find out about the abortion until a year later."

"How long ago was it?"

"A year and a half ago."

"After I talked to you on Friday I called a friend from church—I've known her since high school. She's a volunteer at the crisis pregnancy center. They do post-abortion counseling, and she gave me some insight. I'll go with you, if you want, but I'd like you to meet her."

"Okay." He shifted her in his arms so he could look into her eyes. "There's something I need you to believe, Hailey. I hurt for you, but this doesn't change a thing. I mean. . ." He smiled and touched his thumb to her chin. "It doesn't change how I feel about you."

She nodded and he drew her closer, feeling her conform to his chest. He whispered into her hair, "It doesn't change a thing."

fourteen

An hour later, Cody brushed the back of his fingers against Hailey's cheek, and her eyes fluttered open. She smiled and nestled against him. "How long was I sleeping?"

"Just long enough to imbed this cabinet handle in my back," he teased.

"I'm sorry," she said, without any effort to move.

Cody ran his hand through her hair, letting the long, dark copper strands sift between his fingers. "I'm not."

With a yawn and a cat-like stretch, Hailey sat up and slid off his lap. "Do you still have feeling in your legs?"

He stared at her with an over-done starry-eyed look. "I can't tell—your beauty has numbed me, my love."

"Oh, gag!"

"It's good to hear you laugh again, Little Foot," he said softly.

The tone of his voice brought the pressure of tears behind her eyes again. She stared up at him, folded her arms tightly across her chest, and tried to put words to her feelings. "I was so afraid of telling you."

"What did you think I would do?"

"I don't know. . .but knowing your stand on abortion, I mean, of course you believe in forgiveness, but, oh. . ." she sighed in frustration, "I guess I figured you'd have standards. . ." She looked at him helplessly.

"You assumed I would never consider a serious relationship with someone who'd had an abortion."

Hailey nodded. She was sitting cross-legged next to him, and he sat up straight and folded his legs to match, facing her so that their knees almost touched. He fingered a strand of her long hair that was touching his leg, brushing the ends back and forth against the palm of his hand. Staring down, he said, "And who would I be to condemn you for what God has already forgiven?" He looked across at her. "I have *very* high standards, Hailey. I won't date a non-Christian, and I won't date a Christian who's not truly committed to serving the Lord. I won't compromise my values—I've drawn lines for myself that I refuse to cross, and I won't date a girl that I couldn't imagine marrying someday. But I'm certainly not looking for someone who never makes mistakes!" He shrugged. "There are a few things you need to know about my B.C. days."

Seeing her confusion, he clarified, "'Before Christ.' I was no choir boy! I was smoking pot, on my way to becoming an alcoholic, and I'd been with half a dozen girls before that glorious day when I got my head stuck in the toilet and became a believer!" He laughed at Hailey's wide-eyed expression. "I'm pretty ashamed of all that, but what matters are the decisions I've made since that time."

"Have you. . ." Hailey flushed, not knowing how to finish her question.

"If 'abstained' is the question, the answer is yes. I haven't been with anyone since I was sixteen."

"But how? I mean, with the Lord's help, I know, but . . .thirteen years is so long, and you're so. . ." She blushed under his stare.

"Yes?" He was enjoying her discomfort.

She smiled and made a face. "You're so incredibly. . . *gorgeous*!"

Cody laughed and rubbed the tips of the hair he held gainst her chin. "Thank you. You're pretty easy to look t yourself, you know." He stared at her ocean-blue eyes nd the lips that turned up in a half smile. "I never said it vas easy. One of the lines I never cross is spending too nuch time alone in a pantry with a beautiful woman."

He looked deeper into her eyes, watched the pink rise in ver cheeks, felt his pulse quicken, and took a deep breath. Would you like to go out for dinner? Like, *now*?"

She laughed, stood up, and offered him her hand. "I'd ove to, if you don't mind taking me home first. I only have ny heels, and they don't go with the jeans, and T.J. spilled unch on my dress." She let go of his hand when he was tanding, then turned and walked out of the pantry and nto the kitchen.

"I suppose we'd better lock both doors. I think I got verything put away. There's a ton of leftovers, enough to eed Paige and me and the kids until David and Karlee get ack, but I'll stop over tomorrow and pick all that up." he walked to the front door, locked it, and walked back to ind Cody still standing in the doorway of the pantry, grin- ing at her and shaking his head. She stopped and stared t him.

"Is something wrong?"

"You sure can talk, lady!"

She stopped in her tracks, put her hands on her hips, and ried to glare at him. "Is that going to be a problem? Be- ause if my talking is going to cause you a problem, Dr. Vorth, then I think you'd better say so right now, right up ront, 'cause I don't want it coming up somewhere down he road after I've already fallen head-over-heels for you nd burned all my bridges behind me. So if it's going to be problem, we can just end this relationship, just nip it in the bud before it goes anywhere, before we even get started and. . ."

He took two steps, stopping just inches before her, put one hand on her back and the other on the back of her head, and pulled her into his arms, pushing her face gently into his chest to silence her. Pressing his lips against the top of her head, he said, "It's way too late for that, girl."

❧

The round table-for-two was set in a darkened corner of the Italian restaurant. Hailey slid her finger along the bumpy wax that coated the green bottle in the rattan holder. She stared at Cody's dark eyes through the candle flame, watching the soft light accentuate the angles of his face, the high cheek bones, and the muscles of his jaw line. She pushed aside her half-finished lasagne and traced the red and white squares on the tablecloth.

"You're awfully quiet," Cody said.

She smiled contentedly. "It *does* happen. Occasionally."

"We've covered the bridal shower, the wedding, and the Sparrow Center—now tell me about you."

"What do you want to know?"

"Everything."

"Starting with the day I was born?"

"That'll do, unless you remember anything earlier."

"Well, actually, my parents tell me I was conceived during a snowstorm. . ."

"You don't have to go that far back!"

"Okay. Well, let's see, my dad was in the Marines so we traveled all over until I was about eight. Then we moved to Nebraska and stayed there. I had an uneventful childhood, went to nursing school after high school. . .the rest you've read in my resume."

"I think you must have left out a few details."

"Maybe a couple, my long term memory isn't the best."

"Okay, tell me about recent history."

"Well, about three hours ago I was trapped in a pantry by a tall, dark, and handsome man, and I fell asleep and woke up in his arms."

"I think you left out a few details there, too."

"Yeah, maybe. . ." She pressed her finger into the soft wax just below the candle flame, breaking the dam that held a pool of liquid wax. The stream flowed down the side of the bottle and pooled on the tablecloth. Since she'd been a little girl, she'd possessed the ability to lose herself in the smallest of details when she was trying to shut out the world or fend off disturbing thoughts. But something Randy had said kept coming back to her.

"Have you ever felt that God was cornering you?"

Cody smiled. "Many times."

"I've felt that way the last few weeks, since my interview, actually."

"God cornered you and told you to go out with me, right?"

"Well. . .that was obviously part of it." She smiled across the table. "Could you be serious for a minute?"

He pushed aside his empty plate, moved the candle to the side, folded his hands on the table, and leaned toward her. "I'm all yours."

Hailey took a deep breath. "I guess it really started almost two years ago, but I didn't recognize it—you don't see God's hand in things when you're not even convinced there is a God." She smiled nervously as she poked at the hardening wax on the tablecloth with her fingernail. "I was in this ugly mood for weeks. I'd never gone through a true depression before, where your energy is completely depleted, and you lose your appetite. I sort of prided myself on not being that kind of person, but there I was, dragging around, asking, 'Is this all there is?'

"Anyway, Rachael, this girl I worked with, was convinced that what I needed was the right guy, and her boyfriend just happened to share an apartment with Karlee's high school boyfriend, who I'd secretly had a crush on since I was eleven. To make a long story short, he never knew I was Karlee's sister, we went out, had a great time, got drunk, and ended up at his apartment. Two days later he and his friend left for Texas without a word."

Cody slid his hand over hers. "And you found out you were pregnant."

Hailey nodded. "After the first few days, the denial wore off and I started adjusting to the idea. Then I started even liking it. I sat in the nursery during my break one day, just rocking this little preemie, thinking what a good mother I'd be. I'd seen this little silver music box in the hospital gift shop, and one day on my way out I bought it. I took it home and wound it up and laid it on my belly so the baby could hear it." She pulled her hand away, fumbled in her pocket for a Kleenex, and blew her nose.

"I had this. . .this. . ." she squeezed her eyes shut and fought the sobs that were rising in her chest. Cody rubbed his hand along her arm.

"Take your time," he whispered.

"Sometimes I wonder if I'll ever stop crying." After a few deep breaths she went on. "I had this silly fantasy that Randy would come back in the spring, see me pregnant, and somehow we'd all live happily ever after. The craziest part about it was that I really didn't even know him, and what I did know should have convinced me that he wasn't the husband and father type by any stretch of the imagination!

"It was the first part of December when I found out I

was pregnant, and I went around in that little fantasy world for two weeks, but I still hadn't told anyone. Then one night I was over at Rachael's house when she got a call from Marty, her boyfriend. He wanted her to fly down there after Christmas. She talked to Marty for a while, then she told him to put Randy on. She asked him if he wanted her to bring me along, and then she flipped on the speaker phone so I could hear his answer. He was laughing, I could tell he'd been drinking. . ."

Hailey took another deep breath and stared beyond Cody. "He said, 'No, find me a blond. There's only room in my heart for one redhead.'" Anger flashed in Cody's eyes and his hand moved to her shoulder. She was shaking uncontrollably. Cody stood and took off his sport jacket and laid it over her shoulders.

He picked up the check and pulled his wallet out of his pocket. "Come on," he said, putting his arm around her as she stood, "let's take a walk."

He steered her to a bench beside the river that ran behind the restaurant. Hailey leaned against him, feeling the night air evaporating the tears on her cheeks. "I should have thought about it longer. That's the part I keep playing over and over. There was a doctor that had been at our hospital and then moved to Lincoln, and I knew he did abortions. So I called and made an appointment and made a reservation at a motel because I didn't know if I'd be up to driving home and I didn't want anyone going with me. . .If only I had talked to someone. . .most of my friends probably would have told me to go ahead with it, but I could have called Karlee, or talked to my mother. . ."

Cody tightened his arm around her and rested his cheek on top of her head. "You were scared."

Hailey went on as if she hadn't heard him. "Maybe some

women can claim that they didn't know it was a baby, they can convince themselves that it was just a 'mass of cells' or something, but I'm a nurse, a *pediatric* nurse. I know fetal development, I know my baby had fingers and toes and a heartbeat. . ." Her words were coming in short gasps, and Cody encircled her in his arms, wanting to quiet her, yet knowing instinctively that she needed to get it out.

"I just wanted it over with. I didn't let myself think. I remember turning up the radio on the way to Lincoln, making it so loud I *couldn't* think. I was awake the whole time, and Dr. Mason kept talking to me, asking about people who worked at the hospital, and how the new wing was coming. I remember thinking that he sounded just like my dentist, just like I was getting my teeth cleaned. . ." She covered her face with her hands and sobbed. "There was something so. . .cold about the whole place. I mean, it was sterile and professional, but there was this. . .horror inside me. It was like being raped. . ."

Taking a shaky breath, she leaned closer to Cody, feeling his warmth for the first time. Her voice was softer when she continued. "I took a sleeping pill that first night, and for a long time after that. All the way home, I kept saying, 'It's all over; it's all over.' I must have said it hundreds of times, like a chant. I kept waiting for the relief, but it never came. I put in for a transfer to cardiac the next week, and gradually I just got on with life.

"When my brother-in-law died last May I remember saying and doing all the things I thought I needed to do for Karlee and the kids, but feeling detached, like I was watching myself go through the motions but not feeling anything. Even when my dad had a stroke, I just didn't let myself feel. I guess I was afraid that if I started to hurt again I wouldn't be able to stop.

"In November I came out here to spend some time with Karlee. I was thinking about moving in with her, partly to help her and partly just running, I guess. When I got to Karlee's, Randy was there and things got really ugly. Just seeing him brought it all back, and on top of it all, he was obviously still in love with her. . ."

"Did you tell him about the abortion?"

Hailey nodded and was silent for several minutes. "He finally came back to apologize."

"Good."

"This afternoon."

Cody pulled back and stared at her. "What?"

"He was at Karlee's when I went back to get David's present."

"No wonder you looked like you'd seen a ghost when you got back."

A brief, sad smile crossed her face. "I guess I had." She told him about Randy's visit.

"Is he still around?"

"Randy's not an issue, Cody."

"That doesn't answer my question."

"Yes, he's still around, but he's not a threat. I had a chance to talk to him about the Lord this afternoon. He's searching."

He pulled her close again and smiled. "Very clever. You've found the only reason on earth for me not to tell you to never see him again!" His voice grew serious. "I have to believe that this guy showing up right now is no coincidence. God's working on him. And on you."

"I know. It's like God is hitting me with everything all at once. Like I finally have to deal with it because there's no place to hide."

"Maybe because He has a special job for you."

She smiled up at him, knowing full well what he was implying.

"This is what you call 'Direction with a capital D,' right?"

"Right."

They stared out at the slow moving river, the lamplight swimming in yellow swirls on the surface.

"Cody?"

"Hm?"

"You know what scares me the most?"

"What?"

"Telling David."

Cody nodded. David had lost his first wife and only son while they had been serving as missionaries in Africa. A sudden illness had caused his wife to go into premature labor and they had both died.

Taking her hands in his, Cody said, "Can we pray?"

"Yes," she whispered.

"Lord, thank You for bringing Hailey to this point, and for never letting go of her. This healing may take a while, but I'm just so grateful for Your perfect timing. Give her peace when she talks to David and Karlee—let her love for You be evident to Randy. Lord, in his searching we can already see some of the good You can create even out of our mistakes."

Hailey's voice was low and husky. "This is hard, Lord. I'm learning to accept Your forgiveness, and I believe that Jesus took the punishment for what I did, but it's so hard to forgive myself. Give me the strength I need to do whatever You call me to do." She squeezed Cody's hand. "And thank You, Lord, for giving me this special friend."

fifteen

Watching the dust from Randy's motorcycle drift toward the barn, Hailey slipped the letter into the back pocket of her jeans without reading it. As the roar of the motor dimmed, T.J. walked out of the house, suspicion etched on his face.

"What did *he* want?"

"Just to say good-bye. He was visiting a friend in Chicago. He's on his way back to Nebraska."

T.J. turned away, but not quickly enough to hide the soundless word, "good!"

Not until she reached her room and shut the door behind her did she pull the letter out of her pocket and read it slowly. He said he had written it in case he hadn't found her home, but, from the look in his eyes, Hailey knew he hadn't trusted himself with words.

When she went downstairs several minutes later, a bittersweet sadness was inside her that she pushed away with sheer determination. As she tackled the breakfast dishes, she glanced at the Saturday chore list Karlee had left for T.J. and Shelly, and she felt a surprising eagerness to get on with the day.

"Okay, you guys, front and center this minute! There's a barn to clean, a cat and a dog and a horse and a guinea pig to feed, beds to be made, clothes to be washed. . ." She watched their faces fall. "And a picnic at the park when we're all done!"

"Aw right! I'll take care of Blacky, Shel has to do the

inside stuff!"

Hailey opened her mouth with a comeback when the phone rang. As she answered it, she winked at Shelly and said, "Feed Penny and Mrs. Patches, and we'll take care of him later!"

The sound of Cody's voice brought a strange warmth to her chest. "Hi! Hear anything from the honeymooners yet?" he asked.

"Karlee's called three times already. I don't think she trusts me! Life on the Riviera is just 'divine' she says."

"Ta-ta! So how's things in the aunt business?" he asked.

"Interesting. I was just about to give a lecture on the evils of gender-role stereotyping!"

"Aren't they a bit young for that kind of brainwashing?"

"Rrr! Men! You're going to make some little woman very happy someday."

"Yeah, you're right. Nothin' like comin' home after a hard day at the office to find the wife in a perty little apron . . .I can just smell that homemade pie, fresh from the oven. . ."

Hailey glanced down at Penny's food dish and the charred waffle that had gotten stuck in the toaster. Even the dog wouldn't touch it. "Well, you'd better keep shopping around, mister."

"Hey, you made a pretty tolerable blueberry pie."

Hailey laughed, remembering the wads of failed pie crust that had found their way into the garbage. "Believe me, that was a fluke."

"Well, I don't believe that for a minute, but I just happen to have an offer that will get you out of the kitchen."

"Oh, really. . . ?"

"Yes, ma'am. How would you like to spend a few days in the Montana mountains? Just imagine yourself hiking along the lush green trails, drinking from a crystal clear mountain stream, horseback riding, tubing down the rapids, where big-horned sheep are as common as rabbits, and the black bears eat out of your hand. . ."

"Save your breath for the courtroom. What's the deal?"

"I got a call last night from the private investigator who had been talking to Halona, the woman that runs the art shop. Some guy brought in a couple paintings yesterday morning that he said he'd been given years ago by a local artist and wondered if she would be interested in selling them for him.

"She recognized my mother's signature from our description, so she agreed to take it. She got his name and a post office box. Then about two hours later another guy came in and started asking questions about the first guy, and about my mother. She tried to act like she didn't know what he was talking about and the guy got mad and stomped out. What do you make of that, mystery buff?"

Hailey felt a rush of adrenaline as she thought over the possibilities. "Did he describe the men?"

"No."

"And you didn't ask? How old they were or what they looked like?"

"Not much of a lawyer, am I?"

"I guess not! Okay, here's my theory—these two guys were accomplices in the robbery and they hid the stuff, maybe they found out none of it was worth all that much at the time. Who knows what their motive was in the first place. Anyway, now one of them figured out he could make big bucks off the stuff, and so he moves it where the other guy can't trace him, New Mexico, or somewhere, and the other guy finds out his buddy is making thousands of dollars and he's out to find him!"

"Not bad. That's almost exactly the same scenario the sheriff came up with."

"What? You let me go through all that and you've already got it figured out?"

"Just testing. I had to make sure you really knew your stuff before I asked you to go out there with me."

"You're serious!"

"I'm always serious. Dad and I decided this would be a perfect time to go out for a few days. He's cut his patient load down to about a fourth, and with the Center opening later than expected, it won't be hard for him to get away. And I got to thinking that a change of scenery would do you some good too. Plus, of course, your expertise in mystery solving. If we time it right we might just be there when the 'case cracks.' How 'bout it? Dad bought two tickets, but one more reservation is just a phone call away. David and Karlee get home tomorrow and we'll leave on Monday."

"I don't know. . .wouldn't Paige be the logical one to take along? If they catch these guys and find the paintings, she'd be a big help."

There was a long pause from Cody's end. Finally, he said quietly, "I don't want Paige. I want you."

⁂

Hailey's unplanned Sunday afternoon nap ended abruptly with a nudge from T.J. She was startled to find that she had fallen asleep at the kitchen table. Visions of Montana had kept her awake most of the night.

T.J. was holding the cordless phone out to her. "Mom's on the phone."

"What?" she asked, still dazed. "I didn't hear the phone."

Trying not to sound like she'd been sleeping on the job, Hailey answered. "Hi, Kar."

"Hi! Listen, I'm going to keep this short, 'cause if I start talking now, I won't quit. We just got home and David's on his way to pick up you and the kids and the cat and dog—Paige and I are fixing dinner for all of us and then the two of you can ride home together. Okay? Say yes, I can't wait to talk to you!"

Hailey laughed. "I guess I have no choice!"

T.J. and Shelly were already hauling bags and boxes out to the porch, and Shelly was chattering non-stop. They flew out to meet David's car while Hailey ran to comb her hair and touch up her make-up. She came down the stairs at the same time David walked in to the kitchen. He greeted her with a hug, then held her at arms length, looking at her questioningly. "Are you okay? T.J said Randy was here. What did he want?"

Hailey tried a smile that she knew wasn't convincing. "Oh, he was just passing through."

David's silver-streaked blue eyes stared intently at her. "Nobody just 'passes through' Milbrooke, Wisconsin, Hailey. What did he want? Was he looking for Karlee?"

She fought the tears and hoped the kids would come in and interrupt them, but there was nothing but silence and David's piercing blue eyes. She shook her head. "He came . . .to apologize. . .to me." The tears streaked her cheeks, and David's strong hands eased her into a chair. He waited for her to go on.

Hailey stared down at her hands, feeling them once again in Cody's firm grasp. She remembered his prayer for this moment, and felt the tension in her shoulders weaken. Her eyes brimmed with tears, but there were no sobs. "A year and a half ago. . .I had. . .an abortion. It was Randy's baby. He didn't know until last November. . .when he was here."

There was no response from David, and she was afraid

to look up at him. "This must seem so awful. . .to you."

His voice was soft when he finally spoke. "It *is* awful, Hailey. It's awful that the option of abortion even exists in a civilized country, it's awful that you didn't know the Lord at that time, and that you weren't surrounded by His people."

David put his hand under her chin and lifted it gently until her eyes met his. "Jesus paid for this already, Hailey. He took the lashes and the nails so that you wouldn't have to. Your job is repentance, not punishment. He can't heal your wounds until you put the whip away."

Hailey nodded, and David pulled his hand away and leaned closer. "Karlee said you'd memorized Isaiah 61:3. Think about it: 'beauty for ashes, the oil of joy for mourning, the garment of praise for the spirit of heaviness.' Those are powerful promises."

She took a tight breath. "I know. I guess. . .I can see how God would promise to comfort you, and Karlee, but. . .I caused this. My selfishness took my child's life!"

"If it weren't for human selfishness, Jesus wouldn't have had to give His life. He wouldn't have had to come here at all! Isn't that the root of all sin? And isn't that what grace is all about—undeserved forgiveness for our selfish acts?"

"I guess. . ."

"When we first found out that Shawna was pregnant, my mother suggested that she come home and live with her and my dad until after the baby was born. She could have gotten the proper nutrition and medical care, and she wouldn't have been exposed to diseases that she had no natural immunity to, but I couldn't imagine staying in Senegal without her. I never even asked her what she wanted to do, never took the time to think about what was best for her and the baby. Don't you think I beat myself up with

hat after she died? But I finally had to let it go. I had to get
out of the way so that God could use me again, and that's
exactly what you have to do. Not only can He heal you,
Hailey, He can use you, He can use your mistakes.

"The Sparrow Center wouldn't be opening in two
weeks—it wouldn't even exist—if it weren't for my son's
death. God gave me a compassion I could never have gained
in any other way."

He was silent for a minute. "This is why you don't want
the position Robert offered you," he said.

"Yes. But I guess I have some rethinking to do."

"No.

"It'll be easier once they know. Have you had anyone to
talk to?"

"Just Cody."

"'Just Cody?'" He winked at her and grinned. "They
don't make 'em any better than Cody, sis."

The porch door slammed and they heard the children's
voices.

David stood and held out his hand. Pulling her to her
feet, he wrapped her in a bear hug. As she put her arms
around him, she remembered her wistful comment to Karlee
as they had looked at slides. "I want a David," she had
said. She smiled against her brother-in-law's chest. *You're
right*, she thought, *they don't make them any better than
you and Cody.*

Pulling away as the kitchen door flew open, she smiled
up at him. "Thank you, David."

Later that night, the second in a row without sleep, she
got up and re-read the letter from Randy:

> *Dear Hailey,*
>   *Thank you for taking the time to talk to me.*

*I'll always regret what I did to you. It's hard
to believe that you don't hate me for it. This
whole thing about forgiveness is so strange.*

*Remember what I said about God corner-
ing me? I now believe what you said—there
is no such thing as coincidence. The guy I
went to see in Chicago has a sister who's a
Christian. We stayed up and talked all night.
She read Romans 8:28. I hope something
good comes out of this for you, Hailey. I still
have some questions, but I'm beginning to
see that I can't keep running.*

*Give my love to Karlee. Tell her I wish her
the best.*

Love,
Randy

Hailey folded the paper, wiped her face on her sleeve
and walked to the bookshelf. Gently, almost reverently
she picked up the silver music box and wound it. As the
delicate chimes filled the room, her tears fell again, and
she prayed silently. *Dear God, take care of my baby.
give him to You. I'm so sorry for what I've done, Lord*
*but so grateful for what You have done. I still can't under-
stand that kind of love. Help Randy to stop running, help
him to believe. And thank You, Lord, for Cody and David*
and Karlee and Paige, for their understanding. I love You
Lord.

She folded the letter into a smaller square and placed i
inside the box. As she set it back on the shelf, she had a
sudden certainty that didn't come in an audible voice, bu
was just as real: She would wind the box again some day
for another child.

sixteen

As the wheels left the runway, Hailey's knuckles turned white where they gripped the arms of her seat. She turned toward the window, squeezing her eyes shut and hoping Cody would assume she was absorbed in watching the streets of Milwaukee shrink below them. Though heartfelt, her prayer was more of a distraction tactic than anything. She prayed for a safe flight and for guidance for Cody's journey into his past.

Her eyes were still closed when Cody slipped his hand over hers. She gave him a weak smile, then turned back to the window, concentrating on even breathing until she felt the plane level out. Her attempts at relaxing were hindered by the keen awareness that Cody was intently studying the silhouette of her face against the small window.

"Nervous?" he asked, his lips fighting the curve that would reveal his amusement.

Hailey shifted in her seat, feeling the strength of his hand around hers. "A little, maybe. . .no, a lot."

"Maybe it wasn't such a good idea for you to have the window seat."

"I'm fine. Really. I don't mind *being* up, it's the *getting* up that scares me."

He kept his hand on hers until the "fasten seat belt" light went off above them. Then he released his belt and turned to face her. With exaggerated effort he pried her fingers from the arm rest and placed her hand in his, encasing it between his own large hands. His eyes sparkled as he looked at her.

"Now I realize what a sacrifice this was for you." He squeezed her hand and stopped fighting the grin. "I'm glad you're here—nerves and all."

"So am I. . .but I still think you should have taken Paige instead." She was baiting him and it was obvious to them both.

Pulling his left hand away, he rubbed his chin. "You're right, you know. With all her expertise and connections . . ." He feigned deep thought for a moment, looking past her and out the window, then turned back. "Would you mind taking the return flight back and sending her in your place? I can see I've made a terrible mistake."

With mock indifference, Hailey answered, "That would be fine. I'd much rather be home with a good mystery than taking this silly trip, anyway."

A broad grin erased his dead-pan expression. He locked his eyes on hers and shook his head slowly. "All right, I'll say it. One more time—listen carefully." He mouthed the words slowly and deliberately as if she were deaf and needed to read his lips. His eyes never wavered from hers. "I don't want Paige. I want you."

Hailey laid her head back with a relieved sigh and Cody laughed. "As if you were worried," he muttered, putting his seat back and closing his eyes.

Hailey reached beneath the seat in front of her and pulled a book out of her canvas bag. As she flipped on the reading light, Cody opened one eye. "Another 'who-done-it?'" he asked.

"Mm-hm." She raised one eyebrow and smiled mischievously at him. Though his eyes were still closed, she continued. "It's about a shy, insecure young woman who finds herself on a crime-solving mission purely by accident. You see, it was her beautiful and talented roommate who was supposed to be accompanying the handsome hero, but the mistake wasn't discovered until it was too late, and. . ."

Cody's laugh resounded like the popping of an inner tube, yet he didn't move or open his eyes. The smile still on his face, he spoke slowly through clenched teeth. "Okay. One more time. I. . .don't. . . want. . .Paige. I. . .want. . .you."

Opening her book, Hailey pushed the button on the arm rest that laid her seat back, parallel to Cody's, and let out another long, relieved sigh. Pretending to read, she kept her eyes on his face, watching the smile play on his lips.

He shifted to a more comfortable position and sighed dreamily, still smiling. Hailey was just focusing her eyes on the pages of her book, when she heard his sleepy whisper. "I'm falling in love with a full-blown neurotic."

He opened his eyes just slightly to observe her reaction and was rewarded by the half smile she was trying to hide by biting her bottom lip. He was about to comment when the flight attendant approached them. Looking at Hailey she asked, "Would you like something to drink?"

"No, thank you." Hailey adjusted her seat belt and smoothed out the few wrinkles in her tan blazer and the blue knit shell beneath it as the attendant turned her attention to Cody. She was tall, with long flowing blond hair that she wore loose down her back, pulled away from her face with a leather barrette on top of her head. She had large brown eyes and stunning features that were unusually delicate for her height. Hailey thought of the southwestern appeal she had and tried to read Cody's opinion of the beautiful woman hovering over him.

"Can I get you anything, sir? A cocktail or soda? Coffee or juice?"

"Juice would be fine."

"Grapefruit, orange, or apple?" she purred.

"Anything, grapefruit will be fine."

She set the glass on his tray. "Will that be all, sir?"

Cody nodded.

"Can I get you a pillow or blanket?"

"No," he answered politely.

"We'll be serving dinner soon. If you need anything, my name is Jenna, just ask for me."

Hailey sat staring down at her lap, letting her hair cover her smile, and hoped she wouldn't give way to laughter.

Cody took his glasses off and with his right hand he sought hers and squeezed it. "I know you're laughing, Hailey."

"Coffee, tea, or me, sir," Hailey mocked. "I'm sorry, but she was anything but subtle! Perhaps if she would have offered you some blueberry pie?"

"Are you implying that I could be bought? Maybe. Okay, so maybe your pie influenced me a bit." He winked at her. "But it's not the only way to my heart."

"Thank heavens. I'd be out of the running if it were. It took Paige and me half a day to come up with that poor excuse for a pie."

"It was delicious, and it means even more knowing what a challenge it was!" He smiled teasingly. "It was quite flattering to find two lovely women on my doorstep, giggling like school girls and bearing a pie."

"Didn't you ever wonder why we were there?"

With an indignant look, Cody said, "I just assumed it

was my charm and good looks. . ."

Hailey gave his arm a patronizing pat. "It was just an excuse to get Paige in to see your parents' wedding picture."

Cody attempted a dejected expression. "Oh."

"But you *are* charming."

"Don't forget good looking."

"How could I?"

After a few silent moments, Hailey made a hesitant statement. "I think I could learn to cook."

"I'll give you lessons."

"I'm not sure my fragile female pride could handle that."

"Kill the pride. Do you like Mexican? It's my specialty. I'll teach you to make enchiladas to die for!"

Before she could answer, Jenna appeared to refill Cody's glass. "Would you like more ice?"

"No, thank you."

"Are you sure you have enough leg room? There's an empty seat in front where you could stretch out more."

"I'm fine, thank you."

Across the aisle, a balding man in a gray suit was holding up his empty glass, but only Hailey saw him.

"So, are you staying in Denver, or going on from there?" Jenna asked.

"Heading for Montana," Cody answered. As Jenna turned back to the galley, ignoring the man across the aisle, Cody smiled at Hailey. "Quit snickering. It's not funny."

"Does this happen to you often?"

"Constantly," he said with an arrogant air.

"I was just thinking about your policy of keeping a safe distance from beautiful women. . .Does it still hold?"

"No. I got rid of that policy." He felt the slightest tug as she thought about pulling her hand away from his. Slowly he lifted her hand to his mouth and kissed her fingers. "I could be miles away from you and still not be safe."

The tingling spread from her fingertips to her shoulder, and she fought to clear her head. "I'll wager a home-cooked meal that you don't get off without 'Jenna-dear' slipping you her phone number."

Jenna bent down to make eye contact with Cody as she took their trays away and Hailey wrapped her arm around Cody's. Shaking his head, he laughed at her possessive gesture, then put his table up and stretched.

"I'm feeling bad about Robert sitting alone in coach—after all, I'm the one who's tagging along here," Hailey said. "I should change seats with him—he'd be more comfortable up here."

"Dad would be comfortable anywhere," Cody answered.

"That's true, isn't it? He's so down-to-earth. I've worked with so many doctors that make intimidation an art form—he's different."

Cody nodded. "The man defines the word humility. I'll never forget walking into the foyer of his house for the first time. I was completely blown away—marble floors, flocked wallpaper, an in-ground pool and live-in house-keeper."

"Sounds like a scene from *Little Orphan Annie*."

"Exactly. He'd just kind of forgotten to mention that he was incredibly well-off! He has such a servant's heart."

Hailey paused for a minute. "You're a lot like him, Cody."

He shrugged self-consciously, acknowledging her comment only by squeezing her hand again.

"I remember him caring for my mother in her final stages, while she was still at home. I'm sure I didn't think about it at the time, but I don't ever remember him seeming impatient or tired, even though he was up and down all night. He was so devoted to her."

"I can understand why she fell in love with him," Hailey said softly.

"I guess we both did. I remember him always sitting down to get on my eye level when we talked. And he never hid anything from me—I knew my mother was dying and that I'd be going back to Wisconsin with him. When he adopted me, it was his idea that I keep Wingreen as part of my legal name, and when we moved he had all of my things shipped out here—toys, bed, everything. He didn't ask me to give up a thing."

They were quiet for several minutes, then Hailey asked, "How often did you get back to Montana after you moved?"

"I came back to stay with Millie and Pampa for a few weeks every summer at least. When I moved to Spokane for college I got back more often. I spent most holidays with them until five years ago when Millie died. Pampa went into a nursing home shortly after that and died just a year later. Until then I had no idea they'd willed the shop and cabin to me."

"Cabin?"

Cody sat up slightly. "Haven't I told you about the cabin?"

"No. But I'm listening now."

He winked at her. "You always are." His eyes looked beyond her as he described the rustic cabin on the side of a mountain that had been Millie and Pampa's first home. Leaning against his shoulder, Hailey could almost feel the old boards of the porch swing creaking beneath them, and smell the pine scent in the air as he described it. She could hear the yapping of the coyotes that gradually swelled into an eerie howl in the middle of the night.

"You haven't seen blue sky until you've been to Montana," he added wistfully.

Hailey sat quietly, thinking ahead, sorting through all that she had just heard. "Didn't Pampa and Millie leave anything to their nephew?"

"Not much. He wasn't stable enough to handle much. Lyle was like a rubber check—he'd bounce in and out, always asking for something. Millie and his mother were sisters. After her death his father left—can't blame him—and Millie and Pampa did their best with him. But if there is such a thing as a bad seed, Lyle was it."

"Did anyone question Lyle after the robbery?"

"He would have been an obvious suspect, but he was locked up in the state pen at the time."

Hailey only nodded, feeling suddenly sleepy.

"Why don't you sleep for a bit. I'll go back and talk to Dad for a few minutes."

"Go. I'll be fine."

"Promise you'll miss me?"

"Promise." She rested her head against the side of her seat and watched the clouds swirl past her window until she fell asleep.

⁂

They were met at the Missoula airport by Steve Duncan, the private investigator. Hailey followed Cody down the stairs to the baggage claim, taking mental notes as she went. Karlee would love to hear the details of this quaint little airport—the stuffed black bear in the glass cage, the elk and deer heads mounted near the ceiling, and Canadian geese flying from wires overhead. She also made a mental note not to use the word "quaint" in front of Cody.

Robert and Steve joined them in the coffee shop and introductions were made. Steve appeared to be about forty-five, a large, muscular man. He wore old jeans and boots that had seen several years of wear. In a flannel shirt and blue jean vest, he appeared to be at home here; Hailey saw no hint of the businessman from Sacramento. He drank his coffee black, scarcely waiting for it to cool. Between gulps, he talked fast.

"I rented you a Jeep and booked two rooms at a rustic little inn." He nodded in Hailey's direction. "Should give the lady a good taste of this fine state. Unfortunately, I'm on my way back to California this afternoon. I just got here yesterday, myself, but I got a call this morning that I have to follow up on. I'll fill you in on all I know so far.

"The man that brought the paintings into the shop is nowhere to be found. I haven't talked to anyone who recognizes the description Halona gave, and she had details on this guy right down to the little scar on his left wrist! I just talked to her this morning and she's going to try sketching him from memory. That should help us. The other guy doesn't seem to be trying to keep a low profile at all, but I still don't have much on him. He's been asking questions about Kwanita. A lot of people have talked to him, but no one knows his name or where he's staying. He's not leaving a paper trail, no plastic or checks."

Steve rubbed his hand across the stubble of a two-day beard. "Don't quite know what to make of it. Either he's following the first guy, or they're working together and he's acting as some kind of decoy, trying to throw us off, being elusive, but still visible."

He was plied with questions by the other three until he

was talked out, and it was time for him to catch his plane. He left them with a promise to return before the end of the week.

As they walked out into the bright sunlight, with a view of rounded mountain tops, Hailey remembered something. Shifting her bag to her right hand, she took Cody's hand. "Well, I guess I owe you that home-cooked meal. So much for woman's intuition."

A sheepish expression spread across Cody's face as he pulled his hand from hers and reached into his shirt pocket. Without looking at her, he tucked something into her hand. Hailey let out a low whistle as she opened the folded napkin.

Beneath the airline logo and Jenna's full name was not only a phone number, but also an address.

seventeen

A string of bells on the inside door handle announced their arrival at the shop the next morning. After Hailey was introduced to Halona, a tall, large-boned woman with a heavy black braid down the center of her back, Hailey moved away, letting Robert and Cody catch up on local news.

The room smelled of leather and clay and a spicy-sweet scent that was either incense or potpourri. Combined, it was an earthy, welcoming smell. There was a sense of timelessness in the smooth wood carvings of elk and beaver and the red-brown clay pots. Hailey touched the turquoise band of beads on an elaborate headdress just as Cody came up behind her.

"It hasn't changed much in the past forty years," he said, as if reading her thoughts.

Hailey pulled a pair of silver and agate earrings off a hook and admired them. "I haven't seen any Made-in-Taiwan stickers yet," she said.

"Owner's rules—local artists only. Most of the pottery and the paintings are done right here." He took the earrings from her hand and put them back, then picked up a pair with royal blue stones in a setting of polished copper. "Now these are 'you,' madam. They match your hair and your eyes."

Hailey held one up to her ear and looked in the mirror above the rack. Cody stood behind her, pulling her hair away from her face. "Like 'em?" he asked.

"They're beautiful!"

"They're yours."

"You can't do that!"

"Says who?" He touched his lips to her left ear. "I own the place, sweetheart." He whispered the last word with a Humphrey Bogart twist that ignited tiny nerve endings along her left side.

Her fingers were slow to comply as she tried to remove the earrings she had put in that morning and try on the new ones. When she had them in, she turned around to face Cody. Almost shyly, as though he were afraid to let his eyes linger too long, he took in far more than the earrings: the thin-strapped sandals, blue jeans, red cloth belt, and sleeveless blue denim shirt, the copper lights in the hair that fell over her bare arms. His eyes said all she needed to know. "Thank you," she whispered.

Cody cleared his throat. "I'll show you the back room."

Walking behind him, Hailey forced her eyes away from his broad back and the white cotton shirt that stretched across his shoulders. She concentrated on the charcoal sketches of wolves and oil paintings of bald eagles and wild mustangs that covered the wall to her right.

She followed him into a large, sunlit room with a breath-taking view of the base of a tree-covered mountain. Two potter's wheels took up one corner, while easels dotted the room. A rock polisher was rumbling in another corner. A small adjacent room held a mat cutter and shelves stacked with mat board and wood strips for custom framing.

"This room is new," Cody said. "Now Halona's trying to talk me into making room for a stained glass workshop." Half to himself, he added, "I should just sell the place to her."

"Oh, don't!" She was leafing through the mat board, but stopped, turning to face him with her hands on her hips. "This place is part of you, your heritage, Cody! I mean, you *glow* when you talk about Montana. Your roots are here! Someday you can bring your children here and tell them about their grandmother, and the people they came from. You can take them up to that cabin and tell them all those things you told me, about Pampa building it for Millie as a secret wedding gift, and how they left it to you because you were the grandson they never had, and. . ." Cody was giving her the amused look that was becoming familiar. Her hands dropped to her sides. "I'm doing it again," she said.

He walked over to her, put his hands on her shoulders. "Yes. And don't ever quit."

Hailey lifted her face to him as he leaned closer. At that moment, footsteps echoed off the bare wood floor and walls of the next room. Cody gave her an agonized look and whispered, "Later," before steering her toward the door.

Halona was unlocking a green wooden box that sat below one of the windows and was the size of a small chest freezer. She pulled out two large canvas bags and laid them on the table next to Robert. Cody and Hailey walked in and stood silently behind him. While Cody's eyes were riveted to the two pictures that Halona pulled from the bags, Hailey glanced from the table to Cody's face, and then to Robert.

Robert's expression told her he had no doubt the paintings were authentic. He pointed toward the smaller one. "I don't remember that one, but it's obviously her work, probably something she did long before I met her." He turned to face Hailey, but his eyes went quickly back to the picture. "Kwanita was on her way to making a name for herself while she was still in high school. She turned down an art scholarship when she decided to marry Cody's father. She was twenty-five when I met her and already had quite a few awards to her credit. She had a style all her own, a few more years and she could have—" Robert blinked and shifted his gaze to the larger painting. There was a catch in his voice when he spoke.

"Now this I remember—the view from the cabin. Has Cody told you about the cabin?" Hailey nodded. "Pampa built it, but it was always 'Millie's cabin.' We spent our honeymoon there—I was afraid to take her too far from home. . ."

He took a deep breath and rubbed his chin, as if trying to bring himself back to the present. "I'm rambling. It's just hard to believe she's been gone twenty years when I'm in this place." He stroked the smooth black frame. "Especially with these."

Cody put his hand on Robert's shoulder. "I suppose we should let the sheriff know that we've seen them. He said that once we confirmed that these were stolen, he'd have enough to hold either one of the two men for questioning. Are you worried about having to identify these guys, Halona?"

"I'd be lying if I said I didn't have some qualms about it. I don't think I'd care to see either one of them again."

"You've been a big help, Halona," Robert said. "The sheriff was very impressed with your detailed descriptions."

Her cheeks crinkled when she smiled. "The eye of an artist, you know. Maybe I've done too many wildlife sketches, but that first man reminded me of a weasel from the moment he walked through the door. Beady little eyes. . ."

She shivered and made a face. "He was almost bald on top, with long, greasy hair around the bottom." She gestured as she spoke. "Dirty and scrawny. . .just reminded me of a weasel, or maybe a ferret. His clothes were dirty, and he had long fingernails, black as coal. If he's the one selling Forrest Reed's paintings, he sure hasn't spent any of the money on himself!" She smiled at the look of revulsion on Hailey's face. "Like I said, I wouldn't care to see him again, but I'll identify him if they find him."

"What about the other man?" Hailey asked.

Halona folded her arms and thought a minute. "He was . . .sad, I guess is the best word. I study faces, and before he said a word, I had this sense of sadness, there was something haunting about him. You know how some people just carry the marks of a hard life on their faces? He had a full beard, so I couldn't see much of his face, but very expressive dark eyes. I told the sheriff that even if he was clean-shaven, I'd recognize those eyes."

She stopped and stared thoughtfully at Hailey, then looked up at Cody. Her eyes narrowed slightly, as if trying to picture the man at Cody's age. "I think he must have been very handsome at one time. He walked with a limp, and used a cane, a very unusual cane. It was hand carved, mahogany probably, definitely oriental carvings, and it had a silver head. I was fascinated by him for a few minutes, until he started asking questions. I just played dumb, but I'm sure he could see how scared I was. When I realized he was one of the men who had robbed this place. . ." She shook her head. "I was sure shaking. He got so angry when I didn't give him any information about the other man, I half expected to get hit over the head with that cane!"

The bell on the front door jingled and Halona excused

herself. "I just hope they find those two and the paintings, and we can all just put this behind us!"

"Amen," Robert answered.

While Cody called the sheriff, Hailey followed Robert out to the sidewalk. He stopped in front of the window. "Millie used to change the window display every month with a different theme each time. The last display was in June. . .She was hoping to encourage people to shop for wedding gifts. I remember her asking if it would bother me if she put Kwanita's first wedding dress in the window, and her self-portrait, the one that's in Paige's gallery now. I never had any thoughts of jealousy about Cody's father, but I've often thought that if I'd told her not to do it, they would have stayed upstairs in our apartment—nothing was touched up there. It was the loss of that dress that hurt Kwanita the deepest, I think. Even though she knew how sick she was, she always talked about having a daughter someday. . ."

Robert cleared his throat and put his arm around Hailey. "Well, enough nostalgia for today. We've done the business we came to do; it's time to show you the sights. Has my son shared his agenda with you yet?"

"Agenda? This is supposed to be a vacation!"

Robert laughed. "I promise it will be fun, but if you're hoping to spend some time just sitting around and enjoying the view, you're going to have to get him to cancel something. He's a very organized person."

To herself she said, *Well, opposites attract, they say.* To Robert, she said, "What's on the list?"

"He's already arranged for the dining room at the lodge to pack a picnic, then there's a drive up the mountain to Jed's Point, taking in the view on foot, and then dinner for two at a charming little place overlooking the valley."

"Dinner for two?"

Smiling down at her, Robert squeezed her shoulders. "I have old friends to catch up on."

"But. . ."

"No buts." He dropped his arm and faced her. "I know this is none of my business, but I like the two of you together. You're good for him, Hailey."

She smiled up at him as Cody walked down the front step and enveloped her in his gaze. "He's good for me, too," she whispered.

⋙

Hailey spread a blanket on the grass while Cody brought the wicker picnic basket from the back of the truck. They were in a small clearing, surrounded on three sides by towering pines, overlooking a valley. The rush of water in the river below them echoed off the mountainside. Hailey sat down and unlaced her hiking boots. Three hours earlier they had parked the truck, then explored the hiking trails that wound around the mountain top. She took a deep breath of the clean, crisp air.

"Smell the huckleberry blossoms? They're just starting to bloom about now." He pointed to the steep incline behind them. "We'll walk up and find some after we eat."

Taking off one boot and rubbing her foot, Hailey winced at the thought of more walking, and Cody laughed as he sat down heavily beside her. "Man, I used to be able to climb these hills all day and not get winded or blistered!"

He pointed across the valley. "See that ridge over there, just below that cleared spot? That's where the cabin is. In the fall you can see it from here."

Hailey pulled her knees to her chest and wrapped her

arms around her legs. "Is the cabin on our agenda for the week?"

Cody laughed. "Yes, ma'am, it's scheduled for tomorrow afternoon, but we may have to put it off if we get the rain they're predicting. The road gets a little hair-raising during a thunderstorm."

"Do you rent the cabin out?"

"I've let friends use it for hunting, but no one would care to live there long-term. It's rustic in the true sense of the word—no modern amenities. There's a wood stove for heating and cooking, a few kerosene lamps, and a path out back. But the best artesian water you'll ever taste is pumped right into the kitchen."

"Sounds wonderful. Everyone should have a place like that to escape to."

"It was a God-send while I was going to school. I'd get up here about midnight on a Friday night and sleep till noon, get up and open a can of chili, and take a long walk. There's a little pool about a mile from there. 'Clear as crystal and cold as ice,' Pampa used to say. After climbing around for a few hours, I'd strip my clothes off and jump in. Timing is crucial there, after about ten seconds your heart stops! Then I was ready to go back and stay up half the night studying law books by lamplight like Abe Lincoln."

Hailey sighed. "What a life."

Turning to lean on one elbow, Cody said, "Not everyone would think so. I'm glad you do."

Pulling off her other boot, Hailey laid back on the blanket, hands behind her head, and stared at the sky, intensely aware of Cody, so close she could feel his warmth, still propped on his hand and studying her. "I see why they call this 'Big Sky country,'" she said.

"Mm-hm," he answered.

"And the air even *looks* cleaner. You could forget the whole rest of the world up here!"

"Mm-hm."

"It's so pristine, so untouched and peaceful."

"Mm-hm."

"I wish. . ." She looked over at him and forgot what she was going to say. "I wish you'd quit staring at me!"

"Mm-hm."

"Have you heard a word I've said?"

"Mm-hm."

"Cody!" She had just caught her breath from the hike, but the look in his eyes was making her feel like gasping for air. "Cody. . ." she repeated, a wordless warning in her voice.

She started to sit up, but his hand on her shoulder pushed her gently back to the ground. He put his finger on her lips. "Sometimes, my little motor-mouth, there is a time for silence." He smiled down at her. "Just promise me one thing."

Hailey nodded helplessly.

"Promise me that right after I kiss you you'll push me away and start jabbering again. Otherwise—" He sucked in a long, shaky breath.

Lifting her hand to the back of his head, she whispered the words against his lips. "I promise."

eighteen

The gold and scarlet dawn awakened Hailey just after 6:00 as it danced through white eyelet curtains and onto the matching down coverlet on her bed. She stretched, sat up, then laid back against the pillow, smiling to herself. Her dreams had been laced with images of Cody, but one stood out more vividly than the rest. Closing her eyes, she could still picture him, bare-chested, sitting astride a wild mustang with fiery eyes, flying toward her, black hair feathered in the wind. The horse stopped in front of her, snorting and pawing the ground impatiently as Cody bent down and offered her his hand—and then she had woken up.

She stepped into khaki shorts, then slipped on a loose-fitting olive green sweater over a sleeveless white top. Cody had advised her to dress in layers; though the morning air was crisp and cool, by afternoon the temperature would be in the upper eighties. She taped cotton balls to her heels and eased into socks and boots.

She had just finished putting on a touch of green eye shadow and coral lipstick when room service brought the black coffee she had ordered. She moved the twig rocker and end table over to the wide east window. Settling back into the chair, she thumbed through her Bible, searching for the scripture Cody had shared with her a few days after the wedding. She found Psalms and skimmed until she came to the thirtieth. The last part of verse five read: "Weeping may endure for a night, but joy cometh in the morning. . . ."

She thought of her sister's tears when she had told her about Randy and the abortion. Karlee had grieved with her, holding her in her arms as Hailey had cried again. Hailey's eyes smarted as she thought of the judgement she had expected but never found.

She had talked on the phone for over an hour to Cody's friend who worked at the crisis pregnancy center, and she'd discovered that they shared similar stories. The talk had been healing, and she felt ready to join the post-abortion support group.

She remembered standing in her father's hospital room less than nine months earlier, feeling skeptical as Karlee had prayed for him. *How much things have changed, Lord. You were there through it all, through all the pain and fear. I didn't see You then, but now I see Your hand in everything.* She stared out the window. The colors were leaving the sky, being replaced by a clear, cloudless span of cobalt blue. *"Joy cometh in the morning. . . ."* Thank You, Jesus.

Looking at her watch, Hailey took a last sip of her coffee. She pulled her hair back in a wide gold barrette, then put on the new earrings Cody had given her. She turned her head back and forth as the sunlight picked up the glow of copper. The blue stones didn't go with her green sweater, but, as Cody had pointed out, they did match her eyes.

A knock on the door called her attention away from the mirror.

"Who is it?"

"Room service." It was Cody's voice.

"What did I order?"

"One order of charm and good looks."

Hailey slowly opened the door and peered around it, whispering, "I already have one, thank you."

"Aren't I?"

"Absolutely."

He stood with his hands on the door frame as he had in David's pantry, but this time she savored the feeling of being trapped by him. He seemed to move in slow motion as he bent down and kissed her softly. "Now, Little Foot," he said hoarsely, "let's get downstairs. I'm starving." The expression in his eyes gave his words a double meaning.

Hailey took inventory of the large dining room as she picked up a tray and stood in front of Cody in the buffet line. The tables were pine, polished till they gleamed like glass. They were grouped in concentric half-circles around a massive stone fireplace. One side wall was lined with French doors that lead to a patio with umbrella-shaded tables and a flower garden that, though carefully tended, still had a wild, random look about it. The other two walls were covered with mounted trophies: moose, elk, and deer heads and antlers of various sizes. A bear rug hung above the fireplace and another lay in front of the hearth.

"I feel like I'm being watched," Hailey said.

"Just be thankful you're not a hunter. At least their thoughts of you are only pleasant ones!" He nodded toward the patio. "Think it's warm enough to sit outside?"

"Anything to get away from these eyes!" she laughed.

The patio was terraced into the hillside, overlooking the main street of the little town. They found a table, secluded by trees, but with a view of the store fronts below. As they sat down, Hailey picked up a yellow flier that was tucked between the salt and pepper shakers. "This looks like fun," she said.

Cody glanced at it. "Yeah, but it's not on the agenda."

"Rrrr! Ever heard of spontaneity?"

"Never." He winked, then raised his eyebrows at her plate, barely visible beneath a mushroom and cheese omelet, two pieces of French toast, and Canadian bacon. He thought of how she had only nibbled at a plate of fruit the first day he had met her. "Looks like mountain air agrees with you!"

"I have to keep up my strength to keep up with you!"

Cody prayed and then gave his full concentration to buttering a stack of blueberry pancakes. Hailey picked up her fork, then stopped to look down at the street. "You can see your shop from here! Has the town changed much since you were little?"

Cody nodded, then swallowed and answered her. "It's not much bigger, but it's certainly changed. This lodge is only about ten years old."

Hailey took a bite of her omelet and looked up at him. There was a tenseness in his face that hadn't been there the night before. "Did you sleep okay?"

"Yes—and no. I slept like a log until about four. I was having some pretty wild dreams. I guess that's what woke me up. I didn't sleep too much after that—I'd forgotten just how loud Dad snores."

Hailey thought about telling him her dream, but she quickly changed her mind. "Where *is* Robert? I thought he'd be down here waiting for us."

Cody rolled his eyes as he chewed another bite, then swallowed with a loud gulp. "Are we playing twenty questions again? I thought we'd just sit here and enjoy the morning together, listening to the nuthatches and smelling the honeysuckle."

Hailey laughed, waving her finger in front of him. "No,

no. We've been over this already: I talk. Case closed. So where's Robert?"

Cody smiled, grabbed her finger in mid-air, and kissed it. "He's jogging. We'll meet him for lunch. Now, can I finish eating?"

"No one's stopping you. If a few little questions are going to interfere with your meal, then I think you'd better start eating alone. You know studies have proven that pleasant conversation actually improves diges—"

She stared down at the street with her mouth open. "Hailey?"

"Cody!" she whispered. "Look, coming out of the bookstore. It's him, one of the guys Halona saw in the shop."

"Are you sure?"

"Yes, the salt and pepper beard, wire-rimmed glasses, and the cane—look at the cane!"

"What about it?"

"The silver handle! Weren't you listening?"

Cody shrugged. "Well, if you're sure. . .we should call the sheriff."

But she was already at the top of the steps that led down to the street, motioning for him to follow. "I lost him!" she cried, flying down the steps. She was already across the street in the bookstore, speaking to the teenage clerk, by the time Cody caught up with her.

"Yes, the one in the beard, with the cane. I thought I recognized him. Did he mention his name?"

"No."

"Did he buy anything? Maybe his name was on his check or credit card."

"He bought two books, but he paid in cash." The girl twirled her long black hair around her finger.

"Oh. . ." Hailey pouted and Cody looked at her with raised eyebrows. "I've been hoping to run into him. To be so close and miss him! Did he happen to mention where he was staying?"

The girl, perplexed, shook her head and looked from Hailey up to Cody. Hesitantly she said, "He did ask where he could get a propane tank filled."

Hailey's eyes lit up. "What did you tell him?"

"The gas station on the next corner has—"

Hailey was already at the door. Reflecting the confused look on the clerk's face, Cody thanked her and followed Hailey.

Out in front, she was scanning the street, staring down toward the corner. Cody thrust his hands deep into his pockets and rocked back on his heels. "Well, Miss Austin, I think you missed your calling. The FBI needs you."

She grabbed his hand with an exasperated sigh. "Cody! Don't you know what this means? We have to get the car! He could lead us to the paintings!"

"What we have to do is call the—" He stopped.

"What is it?"

He motioned for her to turn around. They could hear the slam of the trunk from where they stood. Less than a block away, the man stood behind a maroon, late model, two-door Chevy. He held a white propane tank in one hand and a cane in the other.

"Get the Jeep," Hailey ordered. "I'll follow him."

"Yes, ma'am." Cody pulled a pen from his pocket. "Write down the license number—and don't get too close!" He was running across the street as he finished the sentence.

Hailey tried to consciously slow her steps as she walked down the sidewalk, pretending to window shop. When she got close enough to read the number on the license plate, she wrote it down on the palm of her hand, then continued walking slowly past the car and toward the gas station. Before she reached the corner, the man came out of the station, empty-handed except for the cane in his right hand. Hailey took two wide steps to the curb.

The man walked slowly, limping and leaning heavily on his cane, his eyes darting back and forth as he came closer. Hailey's heart was pounding in her throat. She *had* to stall him.

Pointing to the red clapboard depot a block away, she said, "Excuse me, do you know what time the next train comes through?" It was an inane question, but it would do.

"Sorry, I'm not a local." He smiled, and Hailey thought of Halona's first impression. It was a sad smile, strangely haunting, but she didn't know why. She was about to ask him another question when a car horn beeped. The Jeep was across the side street in front of the gas station.

"Thank you, anyway, it looks like I've got a ride. Thank you," she said. He nodded and walked toward his car.

"What were you thinking?" Cody greeted her when she jumped into the car. "You don't stand on the corner and chit-chat with a criminal!"

She shot him an angry look. "Follow him!"

"Okay. But from a distance. And only if you promise to behave yourself."

She smiled coyly and crossed the fingers of both hands so that he could see them. "I promise. Now step on it!"

nineteen

Few cars were on the surrounding roads, and they were able to follow several hundred yards behind the Chevy with no difficulty. They were both silent for the first few miles, until the car turned into a small RV campground. Cody drove past the entrance and pulled off near an abandoned barn.

"I suppose we have a decision to make here." He eyed her nervously, already knowing her answer. "Do we follow him into the park or go call the sheriff?"

"I think we should at least find out where he's staying, and try to get his name from the office. He may be gone by the time the sheriff could get here."

Cautiously, Cody agreed. "That makes sense—but then we find the nearest phone. No heroics, right?"

Hailey's answer was anything but convincing. "Of course." She turned to stare out the back window, straining for a glimpse of the red car.

Cody backed out and turned into the park. He pulled in front of a two-story farm house that was designated as the camp office. Hailey ran up onto the porch and knocked, waited and knocked again.

There was no answer. As she got back into the Jeep, Cody said, "Well, you got the license number, didn't you?" She showed him her hand. "That should be enough to go on. There's a pay phone around the corner."

Hailey looked at him as if he'd sprouted horns. "Co-dy!

141

We have to find out where he's parked!"

Mimicking her tone of voice, he said, "Hai-ley, the guy's already seen you! If he sees you here he'll know you're following him!"

She slunk down in her seat. "Okay. Is this better? You drive, I'll hide."

Cody stepped on the accelerator slowly. As soon as he rounded the first corner he saw the car. "There he is," he whispered.

"Drive past so we can get a good look at the trailer."

Cody eased the Jeep over the speed bumps in the road. Hailey tried to make herself as invisible as possible while still peering out the window. "He's sitting outside! Behind the trailer! Turn around and drive past him again."

"Yes, ma'am."

His voice had an edge of irritation that made Hailey scowl at him, but an idea hit her before she could comment on his attitude. She felt around on the floor until she found her purse, never moving her eyes from the window. She unzipped the outside pocket and fished inside for a folded paper. "Stop!"

Cody slowed to a stop. "We can't just sit here. He'll get—are you *crazy*?" She had opened the door and stepped out before he could grab her. Cody pulled over to the side and parked, then jumped out to follow her, seething, but knowing he had to keep a cool front.

The man was sitting behind his trailer on a lawn chair, with one leg elevated on the bench of a rickety-looking picnic table. Beside him, on a styrofoam cooler, was an open can of soda; an open book lay in his lap. He looked up and smiled as Hailey approached. "Hello! Looking for another train?"

This guy is cool, Cody thought, *too cool*. The anger that rose up in him was sudden and unexpected. He was face to face with the man who had destroyed his mother's final dreams. A cold fear quickly followed. He put his hand on Hailey's shoulder, wanting to grab her and run.

"No. I'm afraid I'm guilty of following you."

Oh, Lord, Cody prayed, *shut her mouth!*

"You mentioned that you didn't live here, so I thought maybe you hadn't heard about this, and I wanted to invite you."

She held out the flyer she had taken off the table on the lodge patio. "I don't know if you're interested in such things, but there's an outdoor Christian concert in the park tonight."

The man stared at the paper with interest, then smiled nostalgically. "Haven't been to one of these in years."

Hesitantly, she asked, "Are you a Christian?"

"Since I was ten years old." He pointed to the flyer. "I used to sing at these things, back in the days when I still had a voice. Played a pretty mean guitar, too."

"Really?" She sat down on the bench of the picnic table.

Cody stood rigid beside her, tugging slightly at her shoulders, but she ignored him. "Where are you from?"

Cody almost smiled, thinking again that she had missed her calling.

"That's a hard one to answer," the man said. "I've been all over. You live around here?"

"No, we're from Wisconsin." She held out her hand, "I'm Hailey Austin."

Cody's fingers pressed into her shoulder. He cleared his throat. "We really need to be going. Hope we see you at the concert. Nice meeting you, sir."

The man held out his hand to Hailey, shook it, and then offered his hand to Cody, who bent forward reluctantly to return the courtesy. "Thank you for inviting me. My name's Richard Wingreen, and I hope we—are you all right?" Cody's hand had gone limp in his.

Cody stepped backward as though he'd been hit. He used his hands to steady himself on the table behind him. Hailey jumped up to put her hand on his back. "Cody, are you all right? Are you sick?"

Cody sat on the bench, stunned, and raked his hand through his hair.

Richard bent forward. "It must be the heat. Can I get you a glass of water or something?"

"I'm okay." He took a deep breath, stood, then sat back down again.

"Cody?" Hailey whispered. "What is it?"

His eyes searched the face of the man in the chair. "My name's Cody Worth, Dakota *Wingreen* Worth. I. . .I think I'm your son."

The man looked confused. "I'm sorry, son, but you've got the wrong man. I don't have. . ."

Cody interrupted him. "My mother was Kwanita Dover Wingreen."

The shock that registered on the man's face was all the confirmation Cody needed. "I was born six months after you were reported killed in action."

Richard stared, his mouth slightly parted, the color drained from his face. The book slid from his lap as he lifted his leg from the bench and eased it to the ground, then leaned closer, his eyes never leaving Cody's face. Tears streamed down his face, into his beard, and he wiped his face with both hands. Finally, he spoke, just above a whisper. "You have her eyes."

He laid his head back and remained quiet for several minutes before going on. "I was shot down over Cambodia, spent some time running and hiding before I was captured, then the prison camp. . .I'd been officially reported as KIA-BNR, 'killed in action, body not recovered,' so no one was looking for me. . ." Hailey felt tears spring to her eyes at the despair in his voice.

"I was in the VA hospital for five years, much of that in a coma." The short account gave no details, but the horror of those years was clearly etched in the lines on his face.

"I tried to reach Nita. . ." His face contorted and he lowered his head. "Her parents told me she had died, but I didn't believe them. Not till I saw the death certificate. . .I asked them about her paintings and they told me they had all been stolen from a store in Edgewater. I didn't believe that either, so I checked with the sheriff's department. . . My health wasn't good for years, or maybe I would have started this earlier. . ." Suddenly, his head snapped up. Anger rang in his voice. "Did her parents know about you?"

Cody nodded. "Yes, they knew, but they never acknowledged me."

"Because of me." The pain that shadowed his face made Cody long to comfort him. He reached out and laid his hand on his knee. Richard took a deep, shaky breath and went on. "They hated me. But to deny me the knowledge that I had a son. . ."

He laid his hand on top of Cody's. "I'm so sorry. If only I had known."

Hailey would have felt like an intruder if Cody hadn't been holding her hand in a vice-like grip the whole time. Gently, she leaned forward and laid her hand on Richard's arm, completing the circle. The gesture seemed to trigger something deep in both men, and the full impact of what they had just gained registered slowly on their faces as they leaned forward to embrace. Cody hugged his father with one arm, still holding tightly to Hailey's hand. As they pulled apart, Richard was smiling through his tears. "God is so good," he said softly.

❧

Hailey sat quietly listening as she watched the cloud shadows move across the mountain tops. For the last half hour, Cody had supplied Richard with every detail he could remember about his mother and what had happened to him since her death. They were only now coming up to the present.

"I own a bookstore in Agoura Hills, California," Richard was saying. "It's near the ocean, not far from Malibu. My employees are all Vietnam vets—mostly friends from the hospital. They all knew about Nita." He looked deep into Cody's eyes. "The Lord saved my life over there, but it was thoughts of her that kept me putting one foot in front of the other. Even after I knew she was. . .gone, I talked about her incessantly for years.

"A few weeks ago, one of the guys ran across a magazine article in some arts publication about Southwestern art. There was a picture of the self-portrait Nita had given me as a wedding gift! I started making phone calls. My only goal at the time was to find that picture, I had no intentions of starting a full-fledged investigation, but that's what it's turned out to be. I've spent more money than I care to think about just on faxes and phone calls. It's become an obsession.

"Last month I finally located one of Nita's paintings in a

gallery in Sausalito. I'd never seen it, but I'd know her work anywhere, and of course it was signed. The price they were asking was beyond my resources, but I left my card and told the owner I was interested in other work by the same artist. He'd already made it clear that he couldn't give me any information on the party he was selling it for. Two weeks later I got a call from some guy who says he has some of Nita's paintings, telling me to meet him on the third of July on the side of a mountain just outside of Edgewater, Montana! Seems strange the guy would be right back where the stuff was stolen in the first place."

Cody nodded and rubbed his chin. "Have you talked to any authorities yet?"

"Not yet. I had no idea it would lead to anything like this. I've been a bit of a crime buff for a long time. I guess I've fancied myself an amateur Sherlock Holmes, or something, but it's finally getting close enough to be dangerous." He looked from Cody to Hailey, and then back again. "I think it's time to let the police in on this."

Hailey had been peculiarly silent for several minutes, but Cody could almost hear the wheels turning in her head. He was not surprised when the questions began to fly.

"Doesn't it sound like he's subconsciously trying to get caught, or like he gets some kind of kick out of flirting with danger, coming back to Edgewater? Does he actually have the paintings with him? Did it sound like he was working alone?"

For the first time, Richard laughed, holding up his hands.

"Wait! I think it's my turn to ask questions again!" He smiled broadly at Hailey, and she suddenly had no doubt about the vague sense of familiarity she'd had when she had met him in town; his smile was the same as Cody's.

"I'll make a deal with you, Mr. Wingreen. We'll answer all your questions if you promise to take us along when you meet with that guy this afternoon."

"Hailey. . ." Cody's voice held a warning.

"I'm not sure that would be wise," Richard said. "We don't want him to think there's a posse after him!"

"I think we should call the sheriff," Cody added.

Hailey gave a compromising smile. "Okay, the sheriff can go with us."

Richard smiled at Cody and shook his head. "You know, they say a man chooses a woman like his mother. . ."

"My mother was never this stubborn!"

There was a glint of tears in Richard's eyes. "You never knew her the way I did. She was as headstrong as they come." He winked at Hailey. "Frankly, I like that in a woman."

With an air of triumph, Hailey turned her back to Cody and faced Richard squarely. "Well, Mr. Wingreen, let's see if we can't sweeten this deal. You mentioned you were trying to find Nita's self-portrait. . ."

Cody grabbed her shoulder. The look on his face was of amused disbelief. "Hailey Austin, that's bribery! Besides, it's rightfully his, anyway!"

Richard leaned forward. "You know where it is?"

With a haughty lift of her chin for Cody's benefit, Hailey turned back to Richard and spoke in a conspiratorial whisper. "Take us along, and it's yours."

twenty

A cold rain began to pelt the metal awning above them as Hailey stood beside Richard, waiting for Cody to return from the pay phone next to the office. Richard shook his head and sighed. "I'm going to have a struggle keeping my eyes on the blessing here. It's hard not to dwell on the 'what ifs.' I had some people from the hospital trying to track Nita down, but she'd moved and hadn't told anyone where she'd gone, all because of her parents. If they hadn't made life so miserable for her. . .

"It hurt to see her married name on her death certificate . . .hard not to hold resentment for the man who shared her last few months, but now—hearing the whole story—I'm looking forward to meeting him. He must be an amazing man."

Hailey nodded and put her hand on his arm. "Cody has two amazing fathers."

"It's going to take me a while to get used to that word. I keep thinking I'm going to wake up any minute."

Hailey smiled at the sight of Cody jogging toward them in the rain, his hair looking even blacker as it pressed against his forehead. She wanted to reach up and push it back, away from his eyes. As if on cue, he ran both hands through his hair and Hailey watched the damp strands slide through his fingers.

"Robert and Sergeant Gorman are going to meet us up there," he said breathlessly. "I just hope they get there in time. It sounds like this guy expects you to follow him. What did he say, exactly?"

"He said to take Ridge Road west from the railroad bridge and look for a green pickup. I asked him how far, but he wouldn't give me any more details."

"Okay. We'd better get moving—here's no way of knowing how far up we have to drive, and it'll be slow going with the rain. I know those roads, I've got a place up there—we'll need four-wheel drive to get up there when it's wet. I think you should drive the Jeep and we'll sit in back," he fixed his eyes sternly on Hailey, "and keep a low profile!"

The sheer drop below the car as they rounded the last bend started Hailey's heart pounding, and the tension in the air accelerated its pace as the Jeep slowed to a stop.

"Are you sure this is it?" Cody asked, a strange look on his face as he stared at the battered, light green pickup truck parked in front of a rustic log cabin.

"It sounds like the one he described. There can't be too many green trucks on this road."

Cody let out a low whistle. "This is too weird—I *own* this cabin!"

Richard turned in his seat, fixing Cody with an incredulous stare. "I'm starting to get spooked about this whole thing." He glanced at his watch, then at the empty dirt road that curved behind them, hoping for a sight of the sheriff's car. "But if I don't go through with this, we may lose this guy for good." He put his hand on the door handle and took a deep breath. "Pray hard and stay low," he whispered as he opened the door.

Hailey gripped Cody's arm as she watched Richard walk slowly toward the truck. The rain had stopped, but the drops still falling from the trees were spattering the windows, blurring their view.

"The truck's empty," Cody whispered.

"He's heading for the cabin."

"This is too weird," Cody repeated.

Richard knocked and the door swung open several inches. Casting a last hesitant look toward the Jeep, he stepped in. Cody's hand slid over Hailey's. "Dear God, protect him."

Hailey looked quickly behind them. "Where is the sheriff? This was really stupid—why didn't we wait for him? What if the guy realizes this is a trap? He's probably armed—we don't even know how many men are in there! Maybe we should do something, cause a distraction or something to give Richard a chance to get away." Her hand found the door handle but was instantly pulled away.

"Now *that* would be stupid! You read too many. . .mysteries."

His last word was barely audible as they watched the cabin door open. Richard stepped out first, followed by a thin man that matched Halona's description. He wore dark blue work pants with a matching shirt, unbuttoned over a stained T-shirt. Hailey felt the same instant revulsion she had felt at the shop. Richard stopped to allow the man to walk down the steps first.

As the man left the shadow of the porch, he looked directly at the Jeep, and Cody suddenly stiffened and gasped. In the next breath, he had opened his car door and was striding toward the two men. Without thinking, Hailey jumped out and ran behind him.

At the sight of Cody, the man froze, then suddenly laughed. "Well, if it isn't the little rich kid! Big-time lawyer by now, I suppose." He turned to Richard. "You two together?" He sneered at Cody. "My prices just went up!"

He laughed again, then stopped as Hailey moved to stand beside Cody. Cody's arm went around her instinctively.

The man leered at her. "Well, well, little rich kid's done all right for himself!" He stepped forward and reached out to touch her hair.

Cody dropped his arm and stepped in front of her. "Touch her, Lyle, and you're dead!"

"Oh, come now, Cody, didn't my aunt and uncle teach you better manners than that? Didn't they teach you to share?"

He took a step to the side, and Hailey leaned closer to Cody. The look in Lyle's small, dark eyes was evil. He reached out for her again, and Cody turned quickly to shield her.

"You haven't done very good at sharing so far, have you? You got the shop, and the cabin, and the rich doctor for a daddy. Doesn't seem quite fair now, does it? Well, I took care of some of that for you. I helped you share, rich boy!" He laughed wickedly and took another step.

"Where are the paintings?" Cody demanded.

"Paintings? What paintings? I was locked up at the time, remember?" He tilted his head to one side, gesturing toward Hailey. "Of course, maybe we could work out a trade. You know, your mother would have done you a big favor if she'd been a little more sharing herself. But maybe you've found a way to make it up to me, hey, rich boy?"

"Back off, Lyle. Get in your truck and get off my property."

Hailey gripped Cody's arm and pressed close to his shoulder. "Stall him!" she whispered.

Lyle's eyes widened, then narrowed quickly. "What's that, sweetheart? 'Stall him'? Is that what you said? You xpecting someone?"

"The sheriff will be here any minute." Hailey was surrised at how her voice steadied as anger replaced her fear.

Lyle laughed. "And what's he gonna do? Arrest me for lirting with a pretty girl?"

"He can start with trespassing, and while they've got ou, you can fill in some details about the robbery."

"So they slap my hand and send me on my way. I've got he best alibi in the world for the robbery." He smiled mockngly at Cody.

Richard, still standing on the porch, stepped down, leanng heavily on his cane. "Marketing stolen property is still felony in this country."

Lyle glanced nervously to the side, and his voice reflected he doubt Richard's comment had created. "I'd like to see hem prove that!"

"I think my shop manager could help out there," Cody aid.

Lylc rubbed the palms of his hands on his pants and icked his lips. "I think maybe it would be best for me to eave. . ." His right hand slid up slowly from his pant leg nd darted beneath his shirt. In one swift movement, he tepped to his right, grabbed Hailey by the arm, and pulled knife from his belt. "But I'm not going alone!" he jeered.

Behind him, Richard lifted his cane silently. Before he ould bring it down, Lyle's foot flew out behind him, hitng him in the leg and sending him to the ground.

Cody grabbed for Hailey, but let go as the six-inch, rooved blade of the hunting knife flew to Hailey's throat. yle, just slightly taller than Hailey, wrapped his left arm cross her chest and started backing toward the truck. Don't try anything heroic, rich boy. It's time for you to accept that you can't have everything! Just consider thi part of my rightful inheritance." He rubbed his face agains her hair and laughed in her ear.

Hailey's breath was coming in short gasps and her hea was beginning to swim. She locked eyes with Cody, th fear in them gripping her. As she stumbled backward, Lyle' heavy breathing seemed suddenly miles away, and th ground began to tilt beneath her. She had almost lost cor sciousness when Lyle slammed her back against the trucl "Get in!" he ordered.

Hailey shook her head to clear it as she crawled onto th ripped leather seat and beneath the steering wheel. She sli across the seat and grabbed for the door handle. It fell o in her hand. Lyle got in and slammed the door, grinning a the terror on her face. He pointed at the handle with th point of his knife. "Neat trick, huh? I knew it would com in handy some day." He gave a cruel laugh and switche the knife to his left hand, then turned the key in the ign tion.

His answer was a series of clicks and then silence. H tried again, swore, and grabbed Hailey's arm. "I gues we'll have to take your car, sweetie. Are the keys in tł Jeep?"

"I. . .don't know."

"You just better hope they are," he warned, pulling h out.

The truck was between them and the cabin, but as the backed toward the Jeep, she could see Cody and Richai over the bed of the pickup. Cody was supporting Richai on his arm, but his eyes were on Hailey. A flash of ligh ning lit up the sky behind them, followed by a rumble th seemed to shake the mountain.

Suddenly, the rain sheeted down on them with such force that Hailey, her head pinned back against Lyle, could not even open her eyes. He pulled the knife away from her long enough to open the passenger door. "You drive," he said, pushing her in.

Her hand shook as she gripped the key. Her boot, caked with mud, slipped off the clutch, and Lyle jumped, pressing the point of the knife against her arm.

"Which way?" she asked.

"You think I'm dumb enough to get trapped at the top of the mountain? Turn around."

The pick-up was blocking the half-circle drive in front of the cabin, so Hailey cranked the steering wheel to the left to make a U-turn. She shifted into reverse, then backed up farther than she needed to, far enough to get a good look at Cody, then inched the Jeep forward.

"Speed it up, sweetie. We don't want to be late for our first date, do we?" He laughed and slid the knife point to the top button of her sweater. "Speaking of our date, I don't think you're dressed quite right." Hailey gasped as the button flew off and hit the window. "Now, isn't that a little better?" The knife slid to the next button.

Please, God, send the sheriff, please. . . The prayer became a chant in her head, the only thing she would let herself think. Twenty yards in front of them was the bend in the road. She turned the windshield wipers to their fastest setting and leaned forward, only to feel the pressure of the knife on her chest. At that moment, the white hood of the sheriff's car eased around the bend. Lyle pulled the knife away and swore again. Hailey breathed a sigh and stepped on the brake.

"Go around him!" Lyle commanded.

"There's no room!"

"Go around him!"

Hailey's eyes swept from the sheriff's car, which had come to a stop, to the sudden drop just yards to her right, and back to the four-foot rock bank on the left.

"Drive around!" There was panic in Lyle's voice. "Now!"

Hailey eased her foot off the brake and stepped on the accelerator. A surge of adrenaline swept through her as she gripped the wheel and wrenched it sharply to the left. The back of the Jeep spun, spitting mud and gravel. Lyle's shoulder crushed against the dashboard as the passenger side slammed into the rock wall on the opposite side, pinning the door against it.

twenty-one

Hailey opened the car door and literally fell into Robert's arms. As he eased her to the ground, she felt Cody's hands beneath her. She smiled to reassure him. "I'm all right," she said weakly.

Robert held his hand up to stop Cody from scooping her into his arms. "I'll be the judge of that," he said gently, as he began deftly checking for injuries. Cody's eyes were wide with fear as he searched her face, then Robert's. "You're sure you didn't bump your head or anything?" Robert asked.

"I'm sure. I'm just a little shook."

"Not surprising. Okay, I guess I'm releasing you into good hands." He winked at her, then nodded to Cody, who pulled her onto his lap. She clung to him and gave in to tears.

Sergeant Gorman was searching Lyle, who was standing spread-eagled against the side of the truck. "Dr. Worth, would you mind having a look at this man while I ask Miss Austin and your son a few questions?" He turned Lyle around and spoke to him as if he were an errant schoolboy. "You know, Lyle, I've got a little more time on my hands these days than I did twenty years ago. When I heard the rumor your face had been seen in town lately, I started doing some research. I had this gut feeling way back then that you had to have been mixed up in the robbery. Revenge is a pretty common motive—revenge for a woman's rejection. . ."

Lyle's eyes narrowed and he spit on the ground. "I was in prison. No way you can tie me to anything."

"Well, I did some checking. . .seems a couple of your cell mates, who just happened to be released two weeks before the robbery, were arrested in Missoula for another armed robbery only three days after the break-in here. Pretty strange coincidence, wouldn't you say, Lyle?"

Wincing under Robert's probing fingers on his shoulder, Lyle's face contorted in a look that made Hailey shiver. "No way you can tie me to *nothing*," he repeated for the third time.

"I'm pressing trespassing charges, Sergeant. He's been staying in my cabin—uninvited."

Sergeant Gorman appeared relieved to have more concrete grounds on which to hold Lyle and began reading him his rights.

Cody pulled Hailey to her feet, then looked at Robert. "You've got another patient up at the cabin. Richard met up with the bottom of Lyle's boot." He turned to the sheriff. "Can the questions wait?"

Sergeant Gorman nodded. Without warning, Cody lifted Hailey into his arms and started walking up the hill, followed by Robert. Hailey struggled feebly.

"I'm all right! I can walk; let me down!"

Planting a kiss on the tip of her nose, Cody gave her a patronizing grin, shook his head, and tightened his grip.

☙

As he watched the back of the squad car disappear around the corner, Cody's fingertips bit into the rough-sawn railing.

From the shadows, Hailey stared at his profile, nervously watching the tight line of his mouth. In the past few minutes, she had watched his light-hearted sense of relief turn to a brooding tension. A thorough search of the cabin had turned up nothing that would connect Lyle with the robbery, no clues to the whereabouts of the remaining pieces of art.

For once, Hailey's gift of words failed her. Hesitantly, she stepped toward him and laid her head against his arm. He exhaled loudly, released the railing, and pounded his fist against the porch frame. "So close," he sighed.

Quietly, almost timidly, Hailey said, "I can't believe that God would bring you this close just to send you home empty-handed. Lyle'll talk."

"They can't force him. He'll be in front of the judge within twenty-four hours, and unless he's drunk up all the profit he's made so far, he'll have no trouble posting bond. They'll set an arraignment date, but he won't show." Cody sighed and bent to touch his cheek to the top of her head. "If I hadn't been such an idiot. . .If I'd stayed in the Jeep, he would have led Richard to *something*, maybe all of it, maybe it's all within miles of here, and the sheriff could have followed him right to it and caught him in the act!"

"Don't blame yourself. He'll talk—I just have this gut feeling that it's all going to work out."

A half smile touched Cody's lips. "I thought *you* were going to solve this one, Nancy Drew."

"I've still got twenty-four hours."

Leaning against a post, his smile faded and he sighed again. "I wish I had your faith." He turned around and sat on the railing, and Hailey took a seat on the bench across from him. Rubbing his temples, he said, "I'm having trouble processing all of this—it's like something out of a bad movie. I used to dream about what it would be like if my father were alive." He closed his eyes, leaning his head back. "It doesn't seem real, somehow. And then Lyle. . ."

Hailey finished the thought for him. "A little boy's nightmare come true."

"And then some. How could anyone be so cruel? Long after she died, he used to talk about her, about how much he had loved her. I hated the times when he showed up."

"Did he know your mother was sick?"

"He must have. I don't know. . .Even so, if he really loved her. . ."

"There's a fine line between love and hate for someone that unstable. At least this gives us a motive—jealousy does horrible things to a person."

Cody nodded. "You know, it's funny, after all this time of hating the memory of those beady little eyes, right now I feel more pity than anything."

Cody stared at the wide planks of the porch floor for several long minutes, then looked up at Hailey. Even in the dim light, he could read the worried expression on her face, and he realized that, for all his teasing about her talking, she was sensing his need for quiet. "I'm glad you're here," he said.

She answered him with a soft smile, and a comfortable silence stretched between them again. The familiar sounds and the soothing presence of the woman sitting across from him took the edge off his gnawing anxiety, leaving an unexpected sadness in its place. He rubbed his hands over his eyes.

Hailey rose quietly and walked over to him. She stood just inches away, but didn't touch him. "You must be exhausted."

He nodded, wishing he had the words to explain what he was feeling. The wasted years, when he could have known his real father, the unfocused anger he'd carried for so long that now had a target, the hopelessness of knowing that

Lyle would walk away and that would be the end of it
. . .But looking into Hailey's face, he suddenly knew that
he didn't need to put it into words. That realization broke
the tight hold he'd kept on his emotions all day. The sting
of tears surprised and embarrassed him, but only for a
moment.

She brushed her hand across his cheek and smiled at
him, a smile that took away his last reserve, then touched
her lips to his damp lashes and laid her head on his chest.
Cody wrapped his arms around her waist and let his tears
fall against her hair.

After a while, he pulled away from her and wiped his
face with the sleeve of his shirt. Cupping her face in his
hands, he kissed the tip of her nose, his eyes searching her
face. "I love you, Hailey."

She pressed her cheek against his hand and closed her
eyes, savoring the words and the warmth of his touch. "I
love you, too."

After a minute, he lowered his hands and picked up one
of her long curls. Winding it around his finger, he lifted it
to his lips. "You look so tired," she said. "Do you trust me
to find us something for supper?"

"I'll even help you," he offered.

"No, you relax. Let me wait on you."

"Mm. My kind a woman. Maybe I'll walk around a bit
while you're slaving over a hot can opener."

"Take your time."

Hailey surveyed the damage in the small alcove kitchen.
Seeing it through Cody's eyes, she felt a strong sense of
violation. A half-empty whiskey bottle and a shot glass
had left white rings on the dark varnished surface of the
small table. The red linoleum counter top was littered with
dirty plates and silverware. She was glad she had told Cody

to take his time. What she needed first was hot water and detergent, then she could think about searching the cupboards for something to fix for dinner.

Standing in front of the cook stove with her hands on her hips, Hailey longed for some of the pioneering spirit that Millie must have possessed as a young bride. She flipped a lever on the stove pipe, hoping she was opening the damper and not closing it. The fire box was stacked neatly with wood and kindling, left, she was sure, by Cody the last time he had been there. She saw no evidence that Lyle had bothered to heat anything that had come out of the tin cans that spilled out of the waste basket. Opening a box of long wooden matches that sat on a shelf behind the stove, Hailey was rewarded by a roar as the wood caught fire and the smoke was sucked up the chimney.

With a smile of satisfaction, she pushed back her sleeves. Taking hold of the worn metal handle of the pump, she thought of the hands that had touched it over the years: Pampa and Millie, Kwanita, Robert, Cody. . .She tried not to picture Lyle in that spot. Remembering her words to Cody as they'd stood in the shop, she wondered if he was entertaining thoughts of selling the cabin, too. She chided herself as uninvited pictures of a Montana honeymoon played in her mind.

After several minutes of pumping, icy water gushed into the sink. Pulling her hair back and re-fastening the barrette that had slipped earlier, she bent over and took a long drink. She filled the largest pan she could find, then emptied it into the copper boiler that sat on the side of the stove.

When the dishes, table, and counter were scrubbed, she began searching the cupboards. Canned peas and corned beef hash would not have been her top choice for the first meal she fixed for Cody, but, she thought with a smile, it was a menu without risk of failure. She put the peas in a small pan near the coolest edge of the stove and the hash in a frying pan near the front. As it heated, she began to sweep the plank floor.

At the opposite end from the kitchen was a high double bed with a massive, carved headboard. As she pushed the broom beneath the bed, she met with a resistance. Lifting the red blanket, she saw the low trundle tucked beneath the bed and pulled it out. She sat down on the worn and faded quilt and imagined Cody as a little boy, curled on the low bed next to Pampa and Millie or his mother. Visions of a third generation filled her thoughts, but were immediately wiped away by the smell of smoke.

Without thinking, she tried to grab the handle of the cast iron pan. Pulling back, she screamed, as much in frustration as pain. Finding a towel, she gingerly pulled the pan to the edge of the stove, and stared helplessly at the charred mass in the bottom. She fought angry tears, kicked at the stove, then walked to the door and heaved it open, propping it with a chair. She hoped Cody wasn't close enough to see the smoke billowing out onto the porch. She looked around, but saw no sign of him.

Working quickly, she set the pan on the porch, rummaged in the cupboards until she found another frying pan and a can of pork and beans, and started over. When the beans were on the stove, she took a towel and flapped it in the air, trying to drive the last of the smoke out the door. Then, picking up the pan, she ran down the porch steps and behind the cabin.

"Time to destroy the evidence!" she whispered.

The ground between the cabin and the rock ledge that towered behind it was carpeted with rust-colored pine needles. Her steps were muffled as she walked to the base of a tree, cleared a hole in the needles with her foot, and began scraped the burned hash into the hole, then covered the remains with more needles. As she turned, she looked up the moss-covered cliff. A pale, pink light played on the wall as the sun, settling behind the mountains, showed its face for the first time since noon and filtered through the branches above her. She leaned the pan against a tree and walked closer, feeling a sense of awe in the hushed, cathedral-like setting.

She was less than ten feet from the base of the mountain before she noticed the pile of rocks just to the side of a low opening, about four feet square. In front of the hole, the bare, muddy spots between patches of needles were covered with footprints.

Hailey smiled, once again imagining Cody as a little boy, sneaking into a secret hiding place. Stealthily, she moved toward the cave, then crouched to enter it, preparing for a surprise attack. *If he were still in there, he couldn't have gone far in the pitch black,* she thought; *like he'd said, though, he knew this mountain like the back of his hand.*

A small chill ran up her spine, the remnant of a childhood fear of the dark. She thought about calling out to Cody, but talked herself out of it. She inched along, bent over, running her hands against both sides of the opening.

Suddenly, the top of her head slammed into a low, squared timber and she fell back, clawing at the walls for support. Two clear thoughts pierced through the pain before she passed out: the "cave" was an abandoned mine shaft. . . and Cody was not there.

twenty-two

She heard her name in a faint, frantic call that echoed through the rock. As she tried to raise up on one elbow, a wave of dizziness knocked her back. Her eyes searched for the opening, but found only thick darkness in every direction. And then she heard her name again, closer this time.

"Cody! I'm in here!" She pushed herself up slowly, stopping to breathe deeply each time her head began to spin.

"Hailey! Thank God! I saw the smoke. . .The door was wide open and. . ."

"The beans! Oh no, I'm sorry!"

"Are you okay? Did they hurt you? Where are they?"

"Where are who?"

"Lyle's partners."

"Cody, make sense!" She rubbed her hand gently over the swelling lump on her forehead.

Cody took a deep breath and tried to steady his voice. "I guess I went a little nuts. All I could think of was what the sheriff had said about Lyle's accomplices. I was sure they'd taken you."

She shook her head and tried to smile. "*Who* reads too many mysteries?" Cody was running the flashlight over her, and the light made the small room spin. "Ooh—move slow. I'm dizzy."

"What happened?"

"I bumped my head and. . ."

Cody was shining the flashlight in her eyes, holding her eyelids open with his fingers.

In spite of her circumstances, Hailey smiled. "Pupils equal and reactive, Doctor?"

"Yes. Thank God." His voice was shaking. He set the light down; the beam hit the ceiling and reflected off the walls. "What were you doing in here?" he shouted. "Don't you know what this is? It's a mine shaft! The roof could have collapsed! You could be lying under twenty tons of rock right now!" He grabbed her by the shoulders. "Don't you ever think before you act?"

Hailey bristled at the anger in his voice and wrenched away from him. "You mean like *you* thought it through before you jumped out of the Jeep?" She glared at him, challenging him with her eyes. "I'm sorry if I'm not *logical* enough for you!" She swept angrily at the tears that covered her cheeks. "I'm sure *someone else* would have handled things better!"

Cody leaned back on his heels. Slowly his lips curved into a smile and he laughed softly. "You are *so* insecure." He reached out and wiped a tear from her chin. Pulling her into his arms, he whispered, "I don't want Paige—I want you."

Hailey nestled against him and cried. "Do I put this in my diary as our first fight?"

"No, this doesn't count. I wasn't really angry, just scared." He tightened his arms around her. "I could have lost you, Hailey. Why did you come in here, anyway?"

"I thought I was following you. When I saw the footprints. . ."

"I haven't been back here. They were probably Lyle's. C'mon, let me get you back to the cabin."

"Cody! Think! They *must* be Lyle's!" She grabbed the flashlight and aimed the beam at the back of the shaft. The tunnel widened in front of them and the light fell on two tarp-covered mounds, each about four feet high.

Hailey handed the flashlight to Cody and crept forward on her knees. Her hand was shaking as she reached out for the tarp. Slowly, she lifted it and heard Cody inhale sharply.

The back of the canvas was toward them. A twisted wire hung over it from two eye-bolts on the wooden frame. In the top, right-hand corner, a penciled inscription read, "Kwanita Dover Wingreen, 8-6-71."

Cody lifted the second tarp. A small, unframed oil painting leaned against a much larger canvas. He picked it up, pointing the flashlight at it: a bald eagle, sweeping up from a glassy lake with a silver fish in its talons; the painting was signed "F. Reed."

Cody shook his head as if to wake from a dream. "Let's leave these for now," he said slowly. "Let the police get fingerprints first."

Several cardboard boxes, covered with clear plastic sheets and taped shut with duct tape, were stacked between the rows of paintings. Cody took out his jackknife and slit open one of the boxes, sliding it in front of Hailey. She opened it and gasped. It was filled with pieces of jewelry. Necklaces, earrings, bracelets, and rings in silver, copper, gold, and pewter. Turquoise, amber, and opal stones caught the light. Hailey ran her fingers through the box and laughed giddily.

Cody lifted a gold necklace with a polished black stone and slipped it over Hailey's head. He lifted her chin with one finger and kissed her lightly. "Part of your reward, my lady."

She grinned up at him like a little girl on Christmas morning. "Open yours!"

"We need to get back to the cabin. Dad will be back any minute." He touched the bump on her forehead. "I want him to check you out. I'll get you settled and come back for this."

"Don't worry about me. Open it!"

She watched quietly as Cody slit the tape. A look of astonishment swept over his face as he picked up something and slipped it over his arm. It was too dark for Hailey to make it out. Gently, he peeled back layers of yellowed paper, then turned to Hailey with a tender smile. Her curiosity taking over, she leaned forward. Quickly, he closed the box. A half smile softened his firm words. "Be patient!"

Giving him a petulant look, she sat back.

For a full, tortuous minute he was silent, ignoring the box and staring deep into her eyes. When he spoke, his voice was hoarse with emotion. "That night . . .when we went to the park after the gallery. . .I think that was when I started falling in love with you. . .you said something . . .about understanding my mother's grief at losing her legacy to me. . ."

Hailey nodded. "You have it now," she said softly.

"And more."

She gave him a questioning look and he answered with a patronizing smile.

Hailey let out a frustrated sigh. "This is torture! What is it? I think you should know that I'm not a very patient person and I hate surprises. I tell everybody what I'm getting them long before Christmas, and I peek at all my presents as soon as they're under the tree. So keeping secrets rom me will only make your life miserable!"

"Are you finished?"

"Maybe."

"Then maybe you wouldn't mind doing something for
ne?"

"What?"

"Close your eyes."

She sighed again, but complied. She could hear the rustle
f the paper, and a shiver of anticipation ran through her.

When he spoke, his voice was little more than a
vhisper. "I want you to have this, Hailey."

She opened her eyes, and then her mouth. Cody was
olding a dress made of soft, white buckskin, trimmed with
lue beads and layered with rows of deep fringe. She stared
ilently for several minutes, touching its softness lightly
vith her fingertips.

"Would you wear it for me someday?"

She closed her eyes, letting the full meaning of his ques-
ion sink in. "When?"

"Soon."

"Is that a proposal?"

"What do you think?"

"I think you want—me."

Cody smiled and kissed the tip of her nose. "Finally. Do
take that as a 'yes'?"

"What was the question again?"

Shaking his head, he asked, "Are you going to make me
et down on one knee?"

She smiled impishly. "No, but I might make you beg a
ttle."

He laid the dress across one shoulder and took her hands
n his. "Hailey Austin, will you marry me. . .please?"

A tear slipped down Hailey's cheek and she leaned into his arms. She nodded against the softness of the buckskin. "Yes," she whispered. "Yes."

After several minutes, he pulled away from her and she finally saw what he had slipped over his arm. The blue beads glowed softly in the dim light. Wordlessly, he pulled the barrette from her ponytail and ran his fingers through her hair, pulling it across her shoulders, then slipped the headband onto her head, sliding it carefully over the bump on her forehead. He smiled and nodded his approval, then tilted her chin with one finger and kissed her. "I love you, Little Foot."

A Letter To Our Readers

Dear Reader:

In order that we might better contribute to your reading enjoyment, we would appreciate your taking a few minutes to respond to the following questions. When completed, please return to the following:

Rebecca Germany, Editor
Heartsong Presents
P.O. Box 719
Uhrichsville, Ohio 44683

1. Did you enjoy reading *Garment of Praise*?
   ❑ Very much. I would like to see more books
      by this author!
   ❑ Moderately
      I would have enjoyed it more if _____

   _____

2. Are you a member of **Heartsong Presents**? ❑Yes ❑No
   If no, where did you purchase this book? _____

   _____

3. What influenced your decision to purchase this
   book? (Check those that apply.)

   ❑ Cover   ❑ Back cover copy

   ❑ Title   ❑ Friends

   ❑ Publicity   ❑ Other_____

4. How would you rate, on a scale from 1 (poor) to 5
   (superior), the cover design? _____

5. On a scale from 1 (poor) to 10 (superior), please rate the following elements.

    ___Heroine   ___Plot

    ___Hero   ___Inspirational theme

    ___Setting   ___Secondary characters

6. What settings would you like to see covered in **Heartsong Presents** books?_____

_____

_____

7. What are some inspirational themes you would like to see treated in future books?_____

_____

_____

8. Would you be interested in reading other **Heartsong Presents** titles?   ❑ Yes   ❑ No

9. Please check your age range:
  ❑ Under 18   ❑ 18-24   ❑ 25-34
  ❑ 35-45   ❑ 46-55   ❑ Over 55

10. How many hours per week do you read? _____

Name _____

Occupation_____

Address_____

City_____State_____Zip _____

Plan the perfect romantic getaway!

From New England to Hawaii and Canada to the Caribbean, **The Christian Bed and Breakfast Directory** has a romantic home-away-from-home waiting for your pleasure. The 1996-97 edition of the directory includes over 1,300 inns that are comfortable, quaint, charming, inexpensive, often historical, and always friendly and inviting. Choose from secluded cabins, beachfront bungalows, historical mansion suites, and much more.

Relevant information about bed and breakfast establishments and country inns is included, inns that are eager to host Christian travelers like you. You'll find descriptions of the inns and accommodation details, telephone numbers and rates, credit card information, and surrounding attractions that satisfy a variety of interests and ages. 576 pages; paperbound; 5 3/16" x 8"

······· Presents ·······

Great Inspirational Romance at a Great Price!

Heartsong Presents books are inspirational romances in contemporary and historical settings, designed to give you an enjoyable, spirit-lifting reading experience. You can choose from 172 wonderfully written titles from some of today's best authors like Veda Boyd Jones, Yvonne Lehman, Tracie J. Peterson, and many others.

When ordering quantities less than twelve, above titles are $2.95 each.

SEND TO: Heartsong Presents Reader's Service
P.O. Box 719, Uhrichsville, Ohio 44683

Please send me the items checked above. I am enclosing $_____
(please add $1.00 to cover postage per order. OH add 6.25% tax. NJ add 6%.). Send check or money order, no cash or C.O.D.s, please.
To place a credit card order, call 1-800-847-8270.

NAME _____

ADDRESS _____

CITY/STATE_____ ZIP _____

HPS 5-96

Hearts♥ng Presents
Love Stories Are Rated G!

That's for godly, gratifying, and of course, great! If you love a thrilling love story, but don't appreciate the sordidness of some popular paperback romances, **Heartsong Presents** is for you. In fact, **Heartsong Presents** is the *only inspirational romance book club*, the only one featuring love stories where Christian faith is the primary ingredient in a marriage relationship.

Sign up today to receive your first set of four, never before published Christian romances. Send no money now; you will receive a bill with the first shipment. You may cancel at any time without obligation, and if you aren't completely satisfied with any selection, you may return the books for an immediate refund!

Imagine. . .four new romances every four weeks—two historical, two contemporary—with men and women like you who long to meet the one God has chosen as the love of their lives. . .all for the low price of $9.97 postpaid.

To join, simply complete the coupon below and mail to the address provided. **Heartsong Presents** romances are rated G for another reason: They'll arrive *Godspeed!*
